INTRODUCING ISSUES WITH OPPOSING VIEWPOINTS®

Drunk Driving

Other books in the Introducing Issues with Opposing Viewpoints series:

Advertising
AIDS
Alcohol
Animal Rights
Civil Liberties
Cloning
The Death Penalty
Drug Abuse
Energy Alternatives
The Environment
Euthanasia
Gangs
Gay Marriage
Genetic Engineering
Global Warming
Gun Control
Islam
Military Draft
Obesity
Racism
Smoking
Teen Pregnancy
Terrorism
UFOs

INTRODUCING ISSUES WITH OPPOSING VIEWPOINTS®

Drunk Driving

Mike Wilson, *Book Editor*

Christine Nasso, *Publisher*
Elizabeth Des Chenes, *Managing Editor*

GREENHAVEN PRESS
An imprint of Thomson Gale, a part of The Thomson Corporation

THOMSON GALE

Detroit • New York • San Francisco • New Haven, Conn. • Waterville, Maine • London

THOMSON
―★―™
GALE

© 2007 Thomson Gale, a part of The Thomson Corporation.

Thomson and Star Logo are trademarks and Gale and Greenhaven Press are registered trademarks used herein under license.

For more information, contact
Greenhaven Press
27500 Drake Rd.
Farmington Hills, MI 48331-3535
Or you can visit our Internet site at http://www.gale.com

ALL RIGHTS RESERVED.
No part of this work covered by the copyright hereon may be reproduced or used in any form or by any means—graphic, electronic, or mechanical, including photocopying, recording, taping, Web distribution or information storage retrieval systems—without the written permission of the publisher.

Articles in Greenhaven Press anthologies are often edited for length to meet page requirements. In addition, original titles of these works are changed to clearly present the main thesis and to explicitly indicate the author's opinion. Every effort is made to ensure that Greenhaven Press accurately reflects the original intent of the authors.

Every effort has been made to trace the owners of copyrighted material.

LIBRARY OF CONGRESS CATALOGING-IN-PUBLICATION DATA

Drunk driving / Mike Wilson, book editor.
   p. cm. — (Introducing issues with opposing viewpoints)
Includes bibliographical references and index.
ISBN-13: 978-0-7377-3621-2 (hardcover)
ISBN-10: 0-7377-3621-6 (hardcover)
1. Drunk driving--United States—Juvenile literature. 2. Drunk driving—United States—Prevention—Juvenile literature. I. Wilson, Mike, 1954–
HE5620.D72D783 2007
363.12'51—dc22   2006031761

Printed in the United States of America

Contents

Foreword 7
Introduction 9

Chapter 1: Is Drunk Driving a Serious Problem?

1. Drunk Driving Is a Serious Problem 15
   Jeanne Mejeur

2. The Drunk Driving Problem Is Overstated 20
   Ed Haas

3. Society Is Too Complacent About Drunk Driving 25
   Rick Popely

4. Society Overreacts to Drunk Driving 32
   Radley Balko

Chapter 2: How Can Drunk Driving Be Prevented?

1. Sobriety Checkpoints Reduce Drunk Driving 39
   National Highway Traffic Safety Administration

2. Sobriety Checkpoints Do Not Reduce Drunk Driving 44
   John Doyle

3. Enforcing Underage Drinking Laws Can Reduce Drunk Driving 49
   Insurance Institute for Highway Safety

4. Chronic Drunk Drivers Require a Comprehensive Approach 55
   National Commission Against Drunk Driving

Chapter 3: How Should Laws Change to Discourage Drunk Driving?

1. A Higher Drinking Age Reduces Drunk Driving Fatalities 63
   Robert Voas

2. The Drinking Age Should Be Lowered *David J. Hanson*	68
3. Lower Blood Alcohol Content Limits Reduce Drunk Driving *Mark Asbridge, Robert E. Mann, Rosely Flam-Zalcman, and Gina Stoduto*	74
4. Blood Alcohol Content Limits Should Be Higher *National Motorists Association*	79
5. Mandatory Ignition Interlock Laws Will Reduce Drunk Driving *Haya el Nasser*	86
6. Interlock Ignition Programs Are Not Always Effective at Reducing Drunk Driving *David J. DeYoung, Helen N. Tashima, and Scott V. Masten*	91
Facts About Drunk Driving	97
Organizations to Contact	101
For Further Reading	106
Index	110
Picture Credits	115
About the Editor	116

Foreword

Indulging in a wide spectrum of ideas, beliefs, and perspectives is a critical cornerstone of democracy. After all, it is often debates over differences of opinion, such as whether to legalize abortion, how to treat prisoners, or when to enact the death penalty, that shape our society and drive it forward. Such diversity of thought is frequently regarded as the hallmark of a healthy and civilized culture. As the Reverend Clifford Schutjer of the First Congregational Church in Mansfield, Ohio, declared in a 2001 sermon, "Surrounding oneself with only like-minded people, restricting what we listen to or read only to what we find agreeable is irresponsible. Refusing to entertain doubts once we make up our minds is a subtle but deadly form of arrogance." With this advice in mind, Introducing Issues with Opposing Viewpoints books aim to open readers' minds to the critically divergent views that comprise our world's most important debates.

Introducing Issues with Opposing Viewpoints simplifies for students the enormous and often overwhelming mass of material now available via print and electronic media. Collected in every volume is an array of opinions that captures the essence of a particular controversy or topic. Introducing Issues with Opposing Viewpoints books embody the spirit of nineteenth-century journalist Charles A. Dana's axiom: "Fight for your opinions, but do not believe that they contain the whole truth, or the only truth." Absorbing such contrasting opinions teaches students to analyze the strength of an argument and compare it to its opposition. From this process readers can inform and strengthen their own opinions, or be exposed to new information that will change their minds. Introducing Issues with Opposing Viewpoints is a mosaic of different voices. The authors are statesmen, pundits, academics, journalists, corporations, and ordinary people who have felt compelled to share their experiences and ideas in a public forum. Their words have been collected from newspapers, journals, books, speeches, interviews, and the Internet, the fastest growing body of opinionated material in the world.

Introducing Issues with Opposing Viewpoints shares many of the well-known features of its critically acclaimed parent series, Opposing Viewpoints. The articles are presented in a pro/con format, allowing readers to absorb divergent perspectives side by side. Active reading questions preface each viewpoint, requiring the student to approach the material thoughtfully and carefully. Useful charts, graphs, and cartoons supplement each article. A thorough introduction provides readers with crucial background on an issue. An annotated bibliography points the reader toward articles, books, and Web sites that contain additional information on the topic. An appendix of organizations to contact contains a wide variety of charities, nonprofit organizations, political groups, and private enterprises that each holds a position on the issue at hand. Finally, a comprehensive index allows readers to locate content quickly and efficiently.

Introducing Issues with Opposing Viewpoints is also significantly different from Opposing Viewpoints. As the series title implies, its presentation will help introduce students to the concept of opposing viewpoints, and learn to use this material to aid in critical writing and debate. The series' four-color, accessible format makes the books attractive and inviting to readers of all levels. In addition, each viewpoint has been carefully edited to maximize a reader's understanding of the content. Short but thorough viewpoints capture the essence of an argument. A substantial, thought-provoking essay question placed at the end of each viewpoint asks the student to further investigate the issues raised in the viewpoint, compare and contrast two authors' arguments, or consider how one might go about forming an opinion on the topic at hand. Each viewpoint contains sidebars that include at-a-glance information and handy statistics. A Facts About section located in the back of the book further supplies students with relevant facts and figures.

Following in the tradition of the Opposing Viewpoints series, Greenhaven Press continues to provide readers with invaluable exposure to the controversial issues that shape our world. As John Stuart Mill once wrote: "The only way in which a human being can make some approach to knowing the whole of a subject is by hearing what can be said about it by persons of every variety of opinion and studying all modes in which it can be looked at by every character of mind. No wise man ever acquired his wisdom in any mode but this." It is to this principle that Introducing Issues with Opposing Viewpoints books are dedicated.

Introduction

"On August 31, 1997, the world was victimized by another drunk driver. Mothers Against Drunk Driving mourns the loss of Princess Diana as well as the other estimated 250 victims killed in our country over Labor Day weekend. Isn't it time we say enough is enough?"

—Mothers Against Drunk Driving

Glamorous. World-famous. Beautiful. Charitable. Often described as the most photographed woman in the world, Diana, Princess of Wales, stunned the world when she was killed in a drunk driving accident in 1997. It was reported that the driver of her car had alcohol in his blood more than three times the legal limit. The day of her death, the world seemed to stand still: People of all nations could barely believe that Diana, a woman who seemed larger than life, could die in such a way. Diana's death was not unusual. In fact, there are more than 2 million drunk driving accidents each year in the United States alone, which result in almost seventeen thousand deaths annually.

The death of Diana provided a shot in the arm to the anti–drunk driving movement. Mothers Against Drunk Driving (MADD) declared that the event be a "wake-up call to Americans" about the loss of life caused by drunk drivers. While the world mourned and eulogized Diana, MADD focused on the involvement of alcohol in the crash. "Although Diana's crash—like virtually all fatal alcohol-related crashes—involved many unsafe contributing factors," said MADD president Katherine Prescott, "the most deadly factor was a drunk driver careening out of control and ultimately robbing the world of 'the people's princess.'" Indeed, Diana's death catapulted the issue of drunk driving into the political spotlight, both abroad and at home.

A controversial and often impassioned topic of discussion, the issue of drunk driving forces society to grapple with the proper balance between roadway safety and the right to drink. Americans think the right to drink is important—it even goes back to the founding of the United States. Seventeenth-century Puritan minister Increase Mather

Police tow the smashed up car in which Princess Diana (left) was killed. The driver had three times the legal limit of alcohol in his blood at the time of the crash.

wrote, "Drink is in itself a good creature of God, and to be received with thankfulness." People aged fifteen and above consumed an average of nine and a half gallons of whiskey a year in 1825, and American soldiers were even given whiskey rations. When the Constitution was amended in 1920 to prohibit alcohol, alcohol consumption did not decrease. Americans simply disobeyed the law, buying liquor from illegal alcohol manufacturers, known as bootleggers, or at illegal drinking establishments called speakeasies. Due to its unpopularity, prohibition was repealed in 1933, and Americans have been free to drink ever since. Indeed, a 2004 poll found that 86 percent of American adults exercise their right to drink alcoholic beverages.

Americans also have a strong interest in roadway safety, driving an incredible 2.87 trillion miles per year, according to a 2002 U.S. Public Interest Research Group report. When so many drink and so many drive, the two will inevitably collide. Tragically, a total of 16,694 alcohol-related fatalities were recorded by the National Highway Traffic Safety Administration (NHTSA) in 2004. Put another way, it is estimated there is an alcohol-related traffic fatality every thirty minutes, and an alcohol-related traffic injury every two minutes. While everyone agrees that drunk driving is a dangerous and undesirable activity, there are disagreements over the best way to reduce it, how it should be punished, and even what constitutes drunk driving.

The main method of determining whether a person is too drunk to drive is measuring their blood alcohol concentration (BAC) level. BAC levels refer to the concentration of alcohol in blood. For example, a BAC of 0.10 percent means there is 1 gram of alcohol per 1000 grams of an individual's blood. Not everyone will have the same BAC level after drinking the same amount of alcohol, however. A person's weight, gender, and the amount of time over which they consume alcohol all factor into their blood alcohol content level. For example, a 260-pound man could drink six beers in an hour and still be legally allowed to drive. His blood alcohol content would be 0.0771 (the legal limit is 0.08 in the United States). Conversely, if a 150-pound woman drank the same amount, her blood alcohol content would be 0.1840—more than twice the legal limit. In general, a person is usually "tipsy" or "buzzed" when they have a BAC of around 0.02 to 0.03. With a BAC of 0.15 to 0.20 they are noticeably intoxicated and are severely impaired. Heavy drinkers tend to lose consciousness at BAC levels between 0.30 and 0.40, and a BAC of 0.50 usually results in death.

BAC Levels

The first BAC levels were established in 1938, when the American Medical Association, along with the National Safety Council, recommended law enforcement to presume drivers to be unsafely intoxicated if their blood alcohol content (BAC) was 0.15 or higher. By the 1970s most states enacted laws that made it illegal to drive with a BAC level higher than a specified level. These early laws established BAC limits ranging from 0.10 to 0.15. Because alcohol-related traffic fatalities continued at an alarming rate, however, anti–drunk driving groups such as MADD successfully lobbied to push BAC limits lower to 0.08, where they remain.

The 0.08 BAC level, however, is contested by those who feel it is too low. The National Motorists Association, for example, claims that most serious drunk driving accidents occur when drivers have a BAC of 0.15 percent or higher. Targeting those with 0.08 percent, they argue, not only unfairly punishes people who have had a cocktail or two and are fit to drive, but also wastes resources on the least dangerous people. They suggest establishing the legal BAC at 0.12 percent to hone in on the most dangerous people. Others, such as Steve Simon, of the Minnesota State DUI Task Force, disagree. In Simon's view, even drivers with a 0.08 BAC constitute a threat on the road. "If .08 percent is good, .05 percent is better," says Simon. "Ultimately it should be .02 percent."

None of the proposed BAC levels, of course, would have saved Diana's life. Her death is sadly one of many that underscore the lone

How Many Drinks Are Too Many?

Drinks Over a Two-Hour Period
One drink equals a 1.5-oz. shot of liquor, a 5-oz. glass of wine, or a 12-oz. beer.

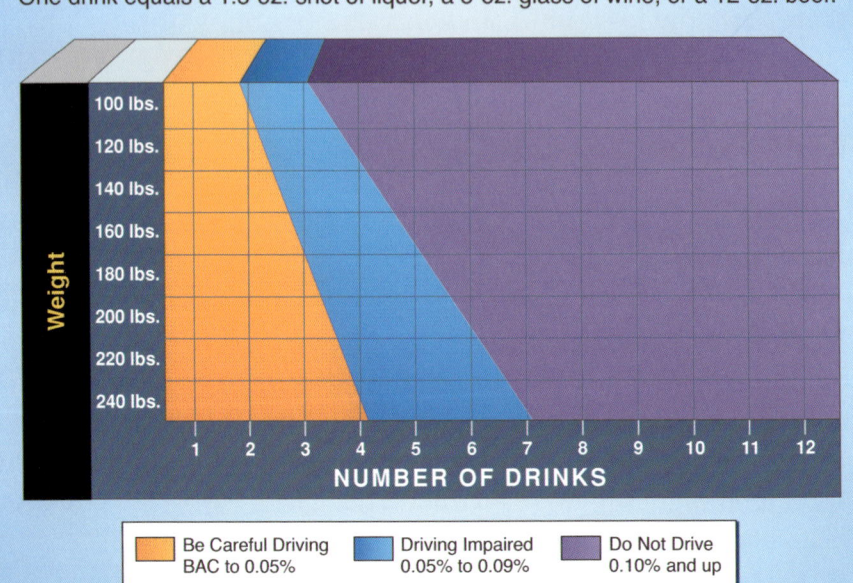

Legend:
- Be Careful Driving BAC to 0.05%
- Driving Impaired 0.05% to 0.09%
- Do Not Drive 0.10% and up

Sources: New Jersey State Police, the New Jersey Department of Law and Public Safety.

truth about drunk driving: It threatens all people, even the young, beautiful, and famous. *Introducing Issues with Opposing Viewpoints: Drunk Driving* covers this and other key discussions related to drunk driving. Through a collection of challenging and compelling essays, readers will learn the basic controversies surrounding drunk driving, how various authors think the problem should be dealt with, and what the newest technologies are for combating this ongoing social problem.

Chapter 1

Is Drunk Driving a Serious Problem?

Approximately 40 percent of all traffic deaths are alcohol related.

Viewpoint 1

Drunk Driving Is a Serious Problem

"Considering the thousands of families affected every year, it's time for a renewed commitment to get hardcore drunk drivers off the roads for good."

Jeanne Mejeur

In the following viewpoint Jeanne Mejeur argues that drunk driving is a serious and persistent problem. Majeur claims that 40 percent of all traffic deaths in 2003 were alcohol related. Many of those deaths involved drivers with blood alcohol concentration (BAC) levels more than twice the legal limit. She argues that drunk drivers are difficult to prosecute because they refuse to take blood tests, which are the single most important piece of evidence needed for prosecution.

Mejeur is a research manager for the National Conference of State Legislatures.

AS YOU READ, CONSIDER THE FOLLOWING QUESTIONS:

1. What percentage of traffic deaths involved drivers with BAC levels more than twice the legal limit, according to the author?
2. According to the author, in which two states do drivers arrested for driving under the influence refuse to take blood tests more than 80 percent of the time?
3. During 2004, according to the author, how many deaths per week were caused by impaired drivers?

Jeanne Mejeur, "Way Too Drunk to Drive," State Legislatures, December 1, 2005. Copyright © 2005 National Conference of State Legislatures. Reproduced by permission.

All are sad stories; some are heartbreaking. Kris Mansfield survived his tour of duty in Iraq, only to be killed by a drunk driver less than four months after coming home to Colorado. The drunk driver's blood alcohol content (BAC) was an extremely high .217.

Seven-year-old Katie Flynn was the flower girl in her aunt's wedding and was riding home from the ceremony when their limousine was hit by a drunk driver going the wrong way on a Long Island parkway. Katie was killed instantly, along with the limo driver. Six members of the family were seriously injured. The drunk driver's BAC was .28.

Forty Percent of Deaths Alcohol-Related

These stories have more in common than a young life tragically cut short. The drivers in both instances were extremely drunk, about three times the legal limit. High BAC drivers are one of the most persistent and intractable facets of the drunk driving problem. . . .

A Vermont state trooper inspects the remains of a car following a drunk driving accident that killed four teenagers.

Of the more than 42,000 traffic deaths in 2003, 40 percent were alcohol related. Twenty-two percent involved drivers with BAC levels in excess of .16. That's twice the legal limit of .08. It's also incredibly impaired.

"High BAC drivers are overrepresented in alcohol-related fatal crashes," says Anne McCartt, vice president for research at the Insurance Institute for Highway Safety. "For this reason, there's nothing misguided about deterrence programs targeting them."

BAC Laws

At least 32 states have enacted high BAC laws, often called aggravated or extreme drunk driving. States with high BAC laws establish a two-tiered system of drunk driving offenses. The basic drunk driving limit is still set at .08 but a second, higher BAC level is established for drivers who are very drunk. States' high BAC thresholds range from .15 to .20.

> **FAST FACT**
> During 2002 one person was killed in an alcohol-related traffic accident every thirty minutes, according to Alcohol Monitoring Systems, Inc.

Some states impose stiffer penalties for a high BAC offense, while others make it a separate offense, with separate penalties. At least 11 states considered bills to establish a high BAC threshold during the 2005 legislative session, but the only bill to pass was in Texas. The new law imposes higher fines and ignition interlocks for drivers with a BAC in excess of .15. . . .

Why Is It Hard to Prosecute Drunk Drivers?

It's hard to prosecute a drunk driver if you don't have a BAC test result. Juries want to know how drunk the driver was. For prosecutors, it's the single most important piece of evidence. It's a big problem, however, because nationwide, about a quarter of drivers refuse to be tested. In Louisiana, Massachusetts, Ohio and Texas, the refusal rate is more than 40 percent. In New Hampshire and Rhode Island, more than 80 percent of allegedly drunk drivers refuse.

In many states, the punishment for refusal is light—generally a license suspension. Compare that to the penalties for a conviction,

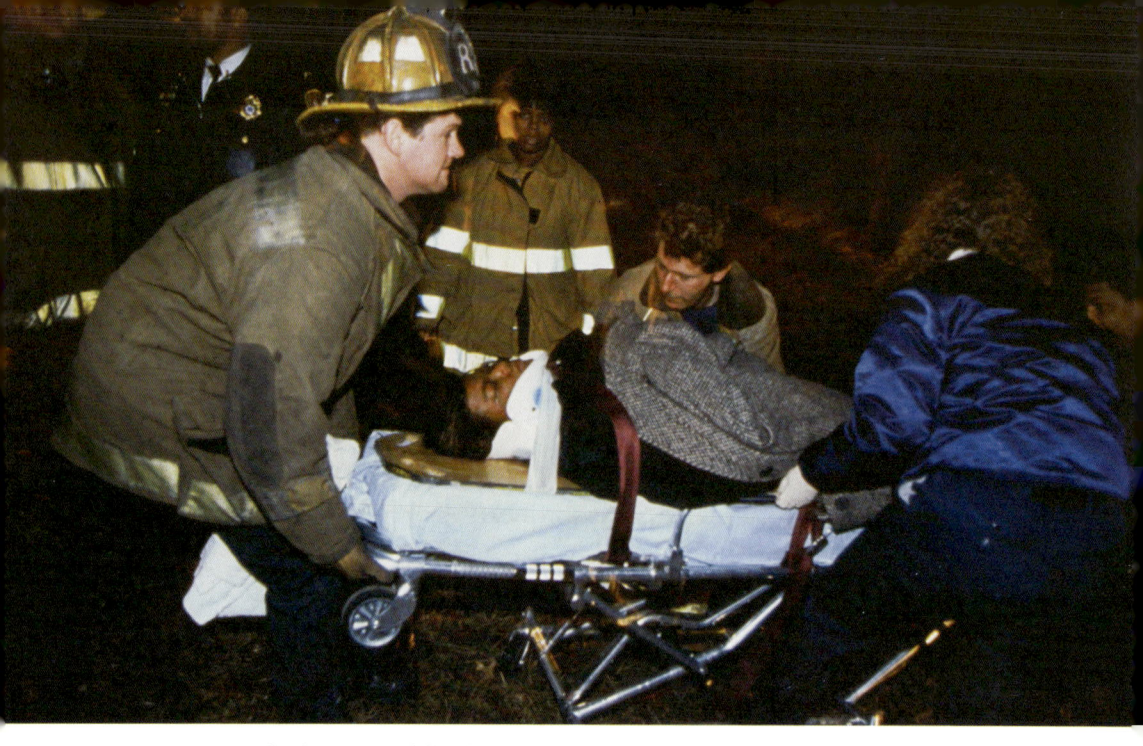

Emergency medical service and fire department personnel help the injured at a car wreck caused by a drunk driver.

which at a minimum include a suspended license, fines, jail time and probation. It's no wonder many drunk drivers refuse the test. . . .

Tens of Thousands of Deaths Per Year and Counting

States have made great progress over the last three decades in reducing drunk driving fatalities. In the past, alcohol was involved in more than half of traffic fatalities. Now it's down to about 40 percent. But there's still a long way to go in reducing drunk driving deaths.

Like those about Kris Mansfield and Katie Flynn, there are thousands of tragic drunk driving stories each year. In 2004, 16,694 deaths were caused by impaired drivers. That's about 320 people a week, roughly the equivalent of a weekly plane crash killing everyone on board. If that were happening, no one would fly and the public would clamor for action. Because drunk driving deaths generally involve only one or two victims at a time and they're spread all over the country, the death toll isn't as obvious as a weekly plane crash. But the number of deaths is the same.

And each story is personal. Glynn R. Birch, national president of MADD, lost his 21-month-old son to a drunk driver. "MADD continues to remind the country that drunk driving should not be tolerated, by placing the faces of loved ones on the cold, hard statistics that litter our roadways," says Birch. Considering the thousands of families affected every year, it's time for a renewed commitment to get hardcore drunk drivers off the roads for good.

> **EVALUATING THE AUTHORS' ARGUMENTS:**
>
> In this viewpoint author Jeanne Mejeur quoted statistics to argue that drunk driving is a serious problem. In the next viewpoint Ed Haas cites a different set of statistics to argue that the problem of drunk driving has been exaggerated. After reading both viewpoints, what is your interpretation of drunk driving statistics? Do they indicate that drunk driving is a serious problem, or not? Explain your answer.

Viewpoint 2

The Drunk Driving Problem Is Overstated

Ed Haas

"The actual percentage of innocent victims of drunk driving is minimal."

Freelance writer Ed Haas argues in this viewpoint that the effects of drunk driving have been blown out of proportion. For example, he argues that the number of deaths claimed to be caused by drunk drivers is exaggerated. When fatalities are called "alcohol-related," he explains, that does not mean that anyone was legally drunk, only that someone involved was believed to have consumed alcohol. In addition, Haas says, the vast majority of people who die in alcohol-related accidents are the drinkers themselves.

Haas is the editor of the *Muckraker Report*, a Libertarian Society news and opinion Web site.

AS YOU READ, CONSIDER THE FOLLOWING QUESTIONS:

1. According to the author, what is the legal blood alcohol concentration (BAC) limit in most states?

Ed Haas, " Misleading Statistics and How Such Have Influenced Our Current DUI Laws and Encouraged the Institution of Suspicionless Seizures Described as Sobriety Checkpoints," *Muckraker Report*, Febuary 15, 2003. Copyright © 2002–2006 by Muckraker Report. All rights reserved. Produced by permission.

2. According to National Highway Traffic Safety Administration statistics cited by the author, in what percentage of alcohol-related fatalities is the involvement of alcohol not verified by testing?
3. According to the author, what is a realistic percentage of substantiated alcohol-related traffic fatalities?

The National Highway Traffic Safety Administration defines a fatal traffic crash as being alcohol-related if either a driver or a non-occupant (e.g., pedestrian) has a blood alcohol concentration (BAC) of 0.01 grams per deciliter (g/dl) or greater in a police-reported traffic crash. To put 0.01 g/dl in perspective, eight times that amount is required to achieve a BAC of 0.08 g/dl, which is now the legal limit of intoxication in most states.

"Alcohol-Related" Is a Loose Term

Simply put, if a legally sober driver is involved in a traffic accident in which another legally sober person is killed, and the person killed

Alcohol-Related Fatalities Are Declining

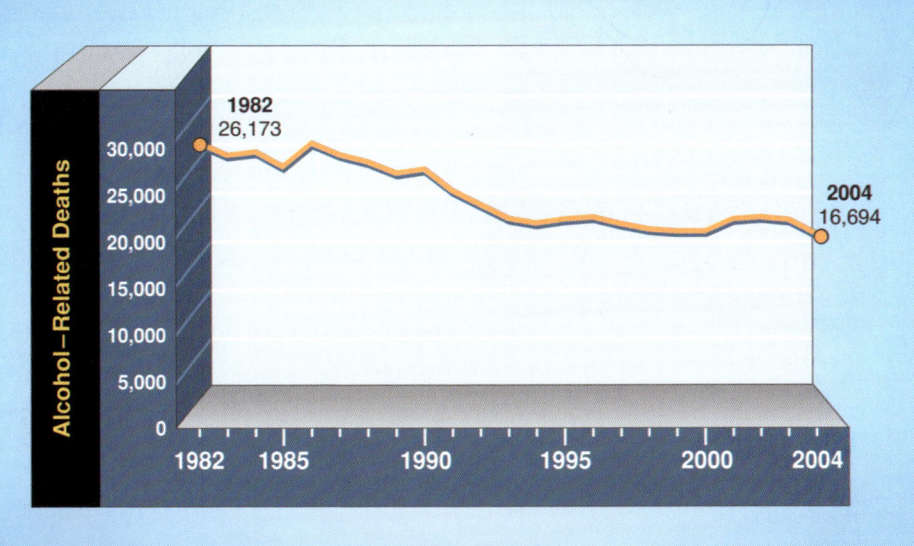

1982: 26,173
2004: 16,694

Sources: U.S. Department of Transportation, National Highway Traffic Safety Administration, Fatality Analysis Reporting System (FARS) database, October 2005.

happened to drink one beer 30 minutes prior to the accident, the NHTSA will classify that fatality as *alcohol-related*. That particular fatality will then be compiled with other *alcohol-related* traffic fatalities, which will then be used by outside organizations such as MADD [Mothers Against Drunk Driving] to fortify the perception that mindless, epidemic-type numbers of drunk drivers are blindly hurling down our highways, aimlessly killing innocent bystanders.

To further illustrate, there were 16,653 alcohol-related traffic fatalities in 2000, according to the NHTSA. Of these 16,653 alcohol-related fatalities, 12,892 involved at least one driver or non-occupant with a BAC of 0.10 g/dl or greater. (In 2000, .10 BAC was the legal limit in many states.) 7,326 were the intoxicated drivers themselves, and 1,594 were legally intoxicated pedestrians and pedal-cyclists. The remaining 3,972 fatalities were non-intoxicated drivers, passengers, and non-occupants.

Statistics Don't Measure Who Was at Fault

Excluding the 7,326 legally intoxicated drivers and 1,594 legally intoxicated pedestrians/pedal-cyclists, there remain 3,972 fatalities—but even these deaths cannot be classified as victims simply because the NHTSA does not indicate which driver was at fault. For example, if a sober driver runs a red light and crashes into a driver who has a BAC of 0.08 or greater, and the sober driver dies, the NHTSA will proclaim that this fatality is alcohol-related, even though alcohol had nothing to do with the accident. Essentially, if alcohol is involved, it is automatically to blame.

Unfortunately, the distortion does not end there. According to the NHTSA, on an average, in more than 50 percent of the reported alcohol-related fatalities, alcohol involvement, as determined by actual alcohol testing, is not known. Alcohol test results may not be known for any of several reasons: the test was given but the results were not obtained by the Fatality Analysis Reporting System (FARS); the test was refused; FARS was unable to determine

> **FAST FACT**
>
> Tobacco causes ten times more deaths than automobile accidents, according to a 2004 *Journal of the American Medical Association* study.

One explanation for reduced alcohol-related fatalities is increased officer patrols and checkpoints.

if a test was given; or, the test was not given. As a result, the NHTSA imputes alcohol involvement in over 50 percent of the reported alcohol-related traffic fatalities. Imputation, as applied by NHTSA, uses characteristics of the persons involved in the crash to predict alcohol involvement when it is not known. Those characteristics include police-reported drinking, age, sex, restraint-use, type of crash, time of day, and driver of striking or struck vehicle. Sadly, these predicted, unsubstantiated, fatalities are masqueraded as confirmed victims of drunk driving, and have had an unjust role in the shaping of DUI laws across America, along with serving as justification to erode the Fourth Amendment protecting against unreasonable search and seizure without probable cause, by the establishment of sobriety checkpoints. . . .

Minimal Innocent Victims

Remember, 50 percent of these fatalities are predicted due to lack of actual alcohol testing. Additionally, approximately 15 percent of the alcohol-related traffic fatalities involve no driver or pedestrian who is legally intoxicated; that one or more of the participants had a measurable amount of alcohol in their blood, but were below the legal limit within their given states. That being said, realistically the percentage of substantiated alcohol-related traffic fatalities is approximately 12.5 percent, with approximately 65 percent of these fatalities being the driver themselves.

Certainly statistics vary from state to state, but rest assured that the same distortion is occurring wherever you may reside. Also, it is important to remember that approximately 65 percent of all alcohol-related traffic fatalities are in fact the driver themselves, so the *actual* percentage of innocent victims of drunk driving is minimal.

As a direct result of this deception, over 1.5 million U.S. citizens are arrested each year for DUI. For over 20 years now, these citizens have fallen victim to the propaganda surrounding their crime, while their respective states inflict unjust punishments upon them.

> **EVALUATING THE AUTHORS' ARGUMENTS:**
>
> In the viewpoint you just read, author Ed Haas argues that the number of innocent victims—those who have not consumed alcohol—in drunk driving accidents is very small. In your opinion should society not be concerned about protecting those who drink from the consequences of their own actions? Why or why not?

Viewpoint 3

Society Is Too Complacent About Drunk Driving

Rick Popely

"Communities need to demand greater enforcement and become more involved in curbing drunken drivers."

In this viewpoint the author warns that society has become complacent about drunk driving. Though tougher laws initially helped bring down alcohol-related auto fatalities, deaths from drunk driving accidents still remain high, he says. Popely worries that the public has lost interest in drunk driving as a social issue and thus communities are not demanding the proper enforcement of drunk driving laws.

Popely is a reporter for the *Chicago Tribune*, from which this viewpoint was taken.

AS YOU READ, CONSIDER THE FOLLOWING QUESTIONS:

1. Why do people ignore drunk driving laws, according to Susan Ferguson of the Insurance Institute for Highway Safety?
2. What percentage of sixteen- to twenty-year-olds are involved in fatal drunk driving accidents, according to the author?
3. To what does Wendy Hamilton, president of Mothers Against Drunk Driving, attribute the lack of public interest in drunk driving?

Chicago Tribune, November 26, 2004. Copyright © 2004 Chicago Tribune Company. All Rights Reserved. Reproduced by permission.

Tougher drunken driving laws and more visible enforcement, such as nighttime roadblocks to check drivers, have helped reduce traffic deaths caused by drinkers. But after falling for 15 years, the percentage of alcohol-related traffic deaths has held steady at a stubborn 40 or 41 percent of the total. Why?

Out of Sight, Out of Mind

"As a country, we've got a short attention span as far as issues," said Wendy Hamilton, president of Mothers Against Drunk Driving. "People believe that the problem is solved. Social issues tend to come and go. It's just not a big issue right now."

In 1982 more than 26,000 people died in alcohol-related accidents, 60 percent of traffic deaths that year. "Alcohol-related" means at least one person involved in an accident had been drinking but was not necessarily legally drunk.

As states adopted tougher laws under federal pressure, the toll from drinking fell to a low of 16,572 in 1999, 40 percent of all traffic fatalities. But alcohol-related deaths increased slightly the next three years before dropping back in 2003 to 17,013, still 40 percent of the total.

Susan Ferguson, vice president of the Insurance Institute for Highway Safety, a research and lobbying group backed by major insurers, says motorists ignore the laws because they do not expect to be caught.

Federal statistics show only 8.5 percent of the drinking drivers involved in fatal accidents last year had prior convictions for driving while intoxicated. Ferguson believes frequent, high-visibility enforcement such as sobriety checkpoints on highways will do more than tougher laws to convince motorists they should not drink and drive.

"It's not about how many people you arrest. It's about how many people you let know that you're out there," she said. "They have to believe they will be caught."

However, state and local police departments are strapped for cash and resources, so roadblocks are often limited to holiday periods, such as Thanksgiving or New Year's.

Laws Aren't Effective Against Alcohol

But some say stepped-up enforcement has done all it can to solve the problem, inducing "social drinkers" to drink less or use designated drivers. It is the problem drinkers who cannot be scared straight.

Wendy Hamilton, the president of Mothers Against Drunk Driving, believes Americans must be reminded that drunk driving remains a serious problem in the United States.

"Most normal people have changed their behavior, but people with alcoholism problems continue to take risks until they get caught or kill someone," says Pat Larson, director of victim services for Schaumburg, Ill.-based Alliance Against Intoxicated Motorists.

Take Lauren Zolecki Polzin, 26, who speaks at meetings organized by the alliance.

She was an underage drinker who frequented bars in McHenry County, Ill., with older friends but never got carded or stopped by police.

"Every time I would wake up in the next morning, I would say I'm not going to do that again," she said of driving while drunk.

Is Drunk Driving a Serious Problem?

"But you don't think about it before you do it. I was a teenager, and I was invincible.

"It's totally normal to drink, but too many people aren't just having a drink or two. I had a drinking problem, though it was not something I admitted to," Polzin said.

Polzin does not remember getting behind the wheel the night in October 1997 when she struck and killed a man who was bicycling home from work in Crystal Lake, Ill. Four hours after the accident, she registered a blood alcohol level of .13, 5 points over the legal limit. She was 19. She pleaded guilty to reckless homicide and served six months in jail.

Generation Y at High Risk

July marked the 20th anniversary of a national drinking age of 21, adopted by states under a federal threat to withhold highway funds if they did not go along.

Nevertheless, 19 percent of drivers age 16–20 involved in fatal accidents are legally drunk, the same percentage as 45–54-year-olds.

Drunk Driving in the United States

The following states have 40% or more of their traffic fatalities come from drunk driving accidents. Rhode Island has the most drunk driving fatalities in the country, with a full half (50%) of its traffic deaths resulting from drunk driving.

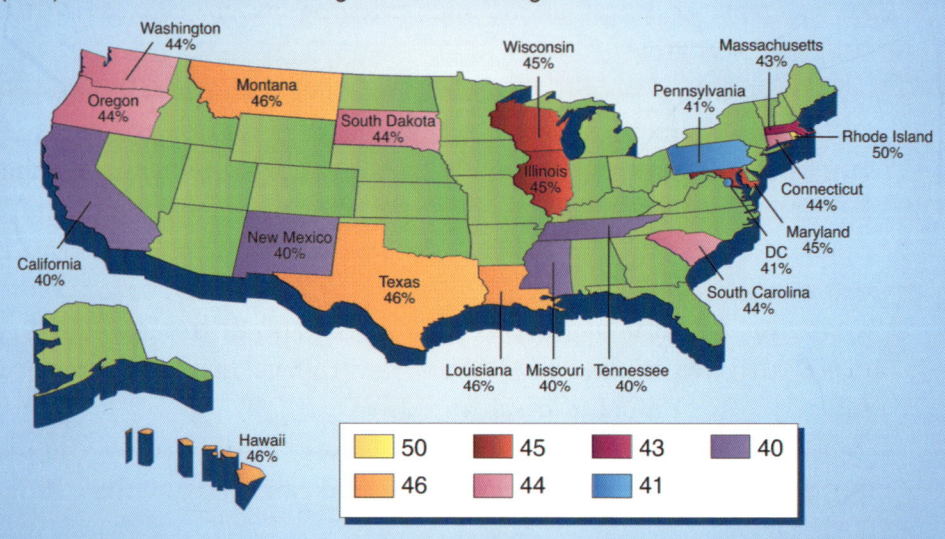

- Washington 44%
- Oregon 44%
- Montana 46%
- South Dakota 44%
- Wisconsin 45%
- Illinois 45%
- Pennsylvania 41%
- Massachusetts 43%
- Rhode Island 50%
- Connecticut 44%
- Maryland 45%
- DC 41%
- South Carolina 44%
- California 40%
- New Mexico 40%
- Texas 46%
- Louisiana 46%
- Missouri 40%
- Tennessee 40%
- Hawaii 46%

Source: National Highway Traffic Safety Administration, U.S. Department of Transportation.

Drivers age 21–24 have the highest percentage of any group, 32, and 25–34 is next highest at 27 percent.

Three-fourths of drivers involved in alcohol-related fatal accidents are younger than 35, the "high-risk years," according to Jeff Michael, director of occupant protection and impaired driving for the National Highway Traffic Safety Administration.

Fast Fact

A DUI conviction in Australia can warrant a fine of as much as $135,000.

One contributor to the decline in drunk-driving deaths in the 1980s and 1990s was that the bulk of Baby Boomers grew out of those risky ages, Michael said.

But all the 165 million to 170 million members of Generation Y are still younger than 30 and could make drunken driving a greater issue.

"Certainly, there is a high-risk age period, and if there are more people in this group, that is going to drive the numbers," Michael said.

Any call for action concerning drunken driving usually includes enacting tougher laws and using stricter enforcement.

Ralph Hingson, a professor at Boston University's School of Public Health, says communities need to demand greater enforcement and become more involved in curbing drunken drivers.

"You have to mobilize a community, not just the police. There has to be motivation within the community for police to vigorously enforce the law," he said.

Elected officials, civic leaders and schools must be involved in a comprehensive effort that includes reducing underage access to alcohol, Hingson said. . . .

Small Fines Don't Deter

Even drivers convicted of a DUI may not be convinced that they have to change their ways.

James Vanek, 42, a recovering alcoholic who now addresses groups on behalf of the Alliance Against Intoxicated Motorists, said he received court supervision and paid "a very small fine" for his first drunk driving offense in 1988, when Illinois' laws were more lenient, and continued to drink and drive.

"I never lost my license for a single day, and I treated it more like a speeding ticket," he says. "It was a non-event in my life."

A police officer gives a suspected drunk driver a sobriety test. Sobriety tests are one method police can use to identify drunk drivers and get them off the roads.

After a third conviction for drunken driving in 2003, Vanek's license was revoked. He cannot get it back for four more years.

Now, he sees the same attitude when he speaks to offenders.

"They're in denial. They're thinking, 'I'm not an alcoholic. I'm not in the same boat as this guy.' I was the same way," Vanek said.

"So instead, I aim at their sense of greed. I tell them about the thousands of dollars it will cost them, the years they will be without a license, how it's going to affect your life."

For his third conviction, Vanek was fined $2,000, paid his lawyer $4,000 and had his Jeep Wrangler, worth about $15,000, confiscated under state law.

Make Drunk Drivers More Responsible for Their Action

Hamilton insists, however, there should be greater focus on convincing motorists to police their own drinking and driving.

"We've done a good job of fixing roads and making cars safer. What we're not doing is building better drivers and addressing the behavioral issues," she said, expressing frustration that the role of drivers in traffic deaths gets little attention.

"God forbid that we point a finger and say that people are to blame."

> **EVALUATING THE AUTHORS' ARGUMENTS:**
>
> In the viewpoint you just read, the author says that many casual or social drinkers avoid drunk driving, but people with alcoholism continue to take risks driving under the influence. In your opinion, how might society go about changing the behavior of alcoholics who continue to drive drunk? Support your answer using evidence from the texts you have read.

Viewpoint 4

Society Overreacts to Drunk Driving

Radley Balko

"Even if the [drunk driving] threat were as severe as it's often portrayed, casting aside basic criminal protections and civil liberties is the wrong way to address it."

Radley Balko argues in this viewpoint that hysteria over drunk driving has resulted in extreme laws that violate civil rights. Balko says that when states pass overly harsh laws against drunk driving, they take away people's rights. In some states, for example, Balko discusses how licenses can be suspended and cars of suspected first-time drunk drivers seized—before they are even convicted. Other states have taken away the alleged drunk driver's right to plea bargain. Some states are even considering installing devices on all cars that make the driver pass a mandatory breath test before driving, which Balko considers to be an invasion of privacy. Balko concludes that drunk driving is not so serious a problem that we should give up our civil liberties.

Balko is a policy analyst with the Cato Institute, a conservative think tank.

Radley Balko, "Drunk Driving Laws Are Out of Control," Cato Institute, July 27, 2004. Reproduced by permission.

AS YOU READ, CONSIDER THE FOLLOWING QUESTIONS:

1. According to Balko, what is misleading about the claim that twenty-five thousand people die in drunk driving accidents each year?
2. Which amendment to the Constitution, according to the author, gives a motorist the right to a jury trial?
3. What does the term "self-incrimination" mean in the context of the viewpoint?

When Pennsylvanian Keith Emerich went to the hospital recently for an irregular heartbeat, he told his doctor he was a heavy drinker: a six-pack per day. Later, Pennsylvania's Department of Transportation sent Emerich a letter. His driver's license had been revoked. If Emerich wanted it back, he'd need to prove to Pennsylvania authorities that he was competent to drive. His doctor had turned him in, as required by state law.

The Pennsylvania law is old (it dates back to the 1960s), but it's hardly unusual. Courts and lawmakers have stripped DWI defendants of the presumption of innocence—along with several other common criminal justice protections we afford to the likes of accused rapists, murderers and pedophiles.

Misleading Statistics

In the 1990 case *Michigan v. Sitz*, the U.S. Supreme Court ruled that the magnitude of the drunken driving problem outweighed the "slight" intrusion into motorists' protections against unreasonable search effected by roadblock sobriety checkpoints. Writing for the majority, Chief Justice [William] Rehnquist ruled that the 25,000 roadway deaths due to alcohol were reason enough to set aside the Fourth Amendment.

The problem is that the 25,000 number was awfully misleading. It included any highway fatality in which alcohol was in any way involved: a sober motorist striking an intoxicated pedestrian, for example.

It's a number that's still used today. In 2002, the *Los Angeles Times* examined accident data and estimated that in the previous year, of the 18,000 "alcohol-related" traffic fatalities drunk driving activists cited the year before, only about 5,000 involved a drunk driver taking the life of a sober driver, pedestrian, or passenger.

Unfortunately, courts and legislatures still regularly cite the inflated "alcohol-related" number when justifying new laws that chip away at our civil liberties.

Taking Away Rights

For example, the Supreme Court has ruled that states may legislate away a motorist's Sixth Amendment right to a jury trial and his Fifth

Driving under the influence charges can result in hefty fines and suspended licenses.

Amendment right against self-incrimination. In 2002, the Supreme Court of Wisconsin ruled that police officers could forcibly extract blood from anyone suspected of drunk driving. Other courts have ruled that prosecutors aren't obligated to provide defendants with blood or breath test samples for independent testing (even though both are feasible and relatively cheap to do). In almost every other facet of criminal law, defendants are given access to the evidence against them.

> **FAST FACT**
> Less than 1 percent of drivers stopped at sobriety checkpoints in Pennsylvania during 2001 were charged with driving under the influence.

These decisions haven't gone unnoticed in state legislatures. Forty-one states now reserve the right to revoke drunken driving defendants' licenses before they're ever brought to trial. Thirty-seven states now impose *harsher* penalties on motorists who refuse to take roadside sobriety tests than on those who take them and fail. Seventeen states have laws denying drunk driving defendants the same opportunities to plea bargain given to those accused of violent crimes.

Newer Laws Are Worse

Until recently, New York City cops could seize the cars of first-offender drunk driving suspects upon arrest. Those acquitted or otherwise cleared of charges were still required to file civil suits to get their cars back, which typically cost thousands of dollars. The city of Los Angeles still seizes the cars of suspected first-time drunk drivers, as well as the cars of those suspected of drug activity and soliciting prostitutes.

Newer laws are even worse. As of last month, Washington State now requires anyone arrested (not convicted—*arrested*) for drunken driving to install an "ignition interlock" device, which forces the driver to blow into a breath test tube before starting the car, and at regular intervals while driving. A second law mandates that juries hear all drunken driving cases. It then instructs juries to consider the evidence "*in a light most favorable to the prosecution*," absurd evidentiary standard at odds with everything the American criminal justice system is supposed to stand for.

Average Cost of a DUI Conviction in Illinois

ITEM	COSTS	FINAL COST
Insurance	High-risk insurance—an additional $15,000 a year. Required for 3 years.	$4,500
Legal fees	Uncontested plea and hardship driving permit.	$2,000
Court costs	Fine of up to $2,500. Court costs—$500. Reimbursements to law enforcement, towing and storage fees—$250. Trauma center fund—$100.	$3,350
Income loss	Loss of 4 weeks' income due to jail or community service, evaluations, and remedial education classes. (Loss based on average yearly income of $40,000).	$4,000
Rehabilitation	Remedial substance abuse class at $50 and counseling fees of $200.	$250
Drivers license reinstatement	$500 plus $10 for a new license; $500 for multiple DUI offenders. $50 formal hearing fee.	$560
	Total Average Cost =	**$14,660.00**

Source: www.cyberdriveillinois.com.

Drunk Driving Hysteria

Even scarier are the laws that didn't pass, but will inevitably be introduced again. New Mexico's state legislature nearly passed a law that would mandate ignition interlock devices on every car sold in the state beginning in 2008, regardless of the buyer's driving record. Drivers would have been required to pass a breath test to start the car, then again every 10 minutes while driving. Car computer systems would have kept records of the tests, which would have been downloaded at service centers and sent to law enforcement officials for evaluation. New York considered a similar law.

That isn't to say we ought to ease up on drunken drivers. But our laws should be grounded in sound science and the presumption of innocence, not in hysteria. They should target repeat offenders and severely impaired drunks, not social drinkers who straddle the legal threshold. Though the threat of drunken driving has significantly diminished over the last 20 years, it's still routinely overstated by anti-alcohol activists and lawmakers. Even if the threat were as severe as it's often portrayed, casting aside basic criminal protections and civil liberties is the wrong way to address it.

> **EVALUATING THE AUTHORS' ARGUMENTS:**
>
> In this viewpoint the author claims that drunk driving is not so serious a problem that we should adopt laws that take away basic civil liberties. Based on your readings so far, how do you think protection of personal rights should be balanced against the dangers of drunk driving? To what lengths should society go to prevent drunk driving? Explain your answer.

Chapter 2

How Can Drunk Driving Be Prevented?

Police use sobriety checkpoints to reduce the instances of drunk driving.

Viewpoint 1

Sobriety Checkpoints Reduce Drunk Driving

National Highway Traffic Safety Administration

"When drivers perceive the risk of being caught is high their behavior changes immediately."

In this article by the National Highway Traffic Safety Administration (NHTSA), the authors argue that the presence of sobriety checkpoints reduces drunk driving. Checkpoints work, says NHTSA, because drivers think checkpoints increase the chance of getting arrested for drunk driving. They therefore do not drink and drive when they know checkpoints are being used. NHTSA says checkpoints should be used often and be highly publicized in order to deter as many drivers as possible from drinking.

The NHTSA is the agency in charge of "You Drink & Drive. You Lose," a government program to reduce deaths caused by drunk driving.

AS YOU READ, CONSIDER THE FOLLOWING QUESTIONS:

1. What did a 1995 NHTSA study in California reveal?

"Small Scale Sobriety Checkpoints," National Highway Traffic Safety Administration, 2006.

How Can Drunk Driving Be Prevented? 39

2. In the Brevard County checkpoint program, according to NHTSA, what type of impaired drivers were stopped?
3. How much does the NHTSA claim the Brevard County checkpoint program decreased alcohol-related traffic fatalities?

Sobriety checkpoints are an effective law enforcement tool involving the stopping of vehicles or a specific sequence of vehicles, at a predetermined fixed location to detect drivers impaired by alcohol and/or other drugs. These operations not only serve as a specific deterrent by arresting impaired drivers who pass through the checkpoints, but more importantly, as a general deterrent to persons who have knowledge of the operation. Sobriety checkpoints increase the perception of the risk of arrest, if they are adequately publicized and highly visible to the public. . . .

High Visibility

The key to deterring impaired driving is highly visible enforcement. Prevention and not arrest is the goal. The research is clear on the effect highly visible enforcement has on deterring impaired driving. When drivers perceive the risk of being caught is high their behavior changes immediately. This is the basis of the *You Drink & Drive. You Lose* campaign. The message is simple, direct, relevant and it works—having already influenced thousands of citizens not to drink and drive nationwide. In most cases, reduced staff checkpoints can be as effective as large scale activities in preventing impaired driving if the effort is correctly publicized to increase the perception of being caught. . . .

> **FAST FACT**
>
> Public opinion polls indicate that 70 percent to 80 percent of Americans favor increased use of sobriety checkpoints.

Checkpoints Work

In 1995, NHTSA conducted a study in six California communities, to evaluate the effectiveness of their checkpoint program's staffing

A driver is placed under arrest after failing a sobriety test at a checkpoint.

levels (three to five officers vs eight to twelve) and mobility (stationary vs three sequential locations).

The principal findings of the report included that the low staffing level approach (when appropriately used) is effective in generating public awareness and it is more cost-effective than a high staffing level configuration. . . .

Success Stories

Some states recently have used techniques that permit them to conduct checkpoints with fewer resources. Moreover, states have found that their small scale checkpoints yielded a number of advantages. Some examples of small scale checkpoint programs are described below:

Pennsylvania

Small-scale, mobile checkpoints expanded the State's DUI enforcement effort over a 15-month intensive enforcement period.

The Majority of States Use Sobriety Checkpoints

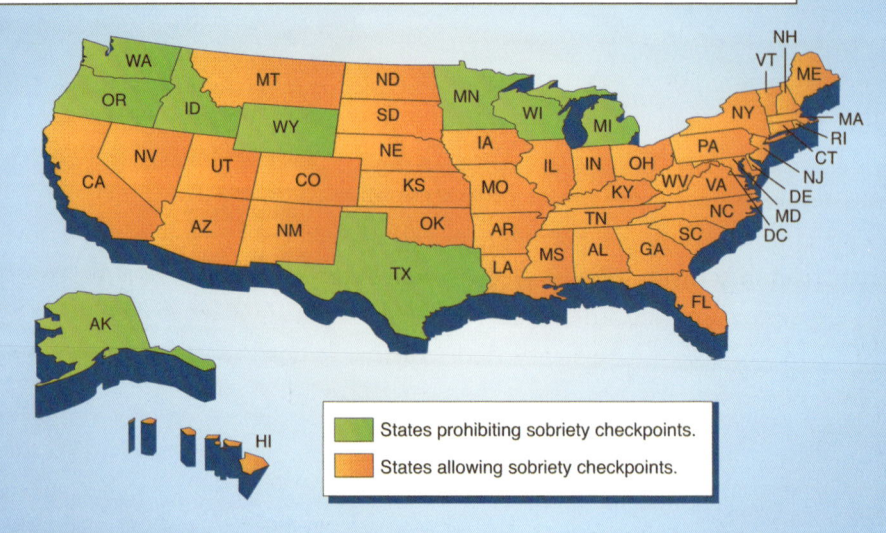

- States prohibiting sobriety checkpoints.
- States allowing sobriety checkpoints.

Source: National Highway Traffic Safety Administration.

Checkpoint activities were run with limited resources, as few as 5 officers. A significant benefit experienced by Pennsylvania's small-scale checkpoints was that they created a heightened awareness of their DUI enforcement program. By allowing the enforcement team to move the location of the operation, within 5-hour periods, the motoring public was encouraged to exercise alternatives to drinking and driving. . . .

Florida

The Brevard County Sheriff's Office initiated Checkpoint Brevard, a program to show that small-scale sobriety checkpoints (using 10 to 12 officers and volunteers as opposed to 35–40) can be an efficient way to apprehend impaired drivers. The operational plan included involving officers from other jurisdictions . . . , media events (press conferences & live feeds), and rotating checkpoints to high crash locations. Officers participating in Checkpoint Brevard made 163 impaired driving arrests over a two-year period. In addition, 58 persons were arrested on drug charges, 20 arrested on felony charges and 115 arrested for other misdemeanor offenses. Checkpoint Brevard produced a significant decrease in alcohol-related traffic fatalities

(38.2%), and a decrease in alcohol-related crashes with injury (9.3%). Officer and public safety did not appear to be affected negatively by using less manpower at the checkpoints. At 37 checkpoints, not one crash took place. Small-scale checkpoints are now being conducted on a monthly basis. . . .

Checkpoints Are Legal

The U.S. Supreme Court in 1990 (*Michigan v. Sitz*) upheld the constitutionality of sobriety checkpoints. The Court held that the interest in reducing alcohol-impaired driving was sufficient to justify the brief intrusion of a sobriety checkpoint. If conducted properly, sobriety checkpoints do not constitute illegal search and seizure in most states.

EVALUATING THE AUTHORS' ARGUMENTS:

In this viewpoint the author argues that sobriety checkpoints reduce drunk driving. The author of the following viewpoint disagrees. After reading both viewpoints, with which author do you agree on the effectiveness of sobriety checkpoints at reducing drunk driving? Support your answer using evidence from the texts.

Viewpoint 2

Sobriety Checkpoints Do Not Reduce Drunk Driving

John Doyle

"Targeted enforcement —not roadblocks designed to snare the wrong people—saves lives."

In this viewpoint John Doyle argues that sobriety checkpoints are not the most effective way to reduce drunk driving. Instead, he suggests that roving police patrols prevent drunk driving accidents better than sobriety checkpoints because they target drivers too drunk to drive safely. Doyle says that sobriety checkpoints infringe on people because they target everyone who drinks and drives, even if they pose no danger to others. He also argues that chronic drunk drivers, who are the real danger to other drivers, avoid publicized roadblocks.

Doyle is executive director of the American Beverage Institute.

AS YOU READ, CONSIDER THE FOLLOWING QUESTIONS:

1. According to the author, how many Americans drink responsibly?
2. What does the author say can be learned from the eleven states that do not use roadblocks?

John Doyle, "Sobriety Checkpoints Are Intrusive and Wasteful," *The Record*, December 19, 2005. Copyright © Bergen Record Corporation. Reproduced by permission of the author.

3. What did the National Highway Traffic Safety Administration find about roving police patrols?

When most of us think of the holidays, we think of gathering together in the company of friends and family, perhaps drinking eggnog and roasting chestnuts over an open fire. These days, however, that glass of eggnog (assuming it's the real stuff) could get you in trouble. That's because during the holiday season, sobriety checkpoints will be as ubiquitous as the inexplicable presence of fruitcake at holiday parties.

"Checkpoints," you say? "Like they had at the Berlin Wall?" Not exactly. That one was fixed, whereas these are entirely random. The police will set up roadblocks at various positions from which they will indiscriminately stop drivers, shine flashlights in their faces and assess the driver's level of sobriety.

However, they will no longer simply be checking to ensure that drivers are below the legal limit of .08 percent blood alcohol content. Secretary of Transportation Norman Mineta announced in 2003 that

"This is just a routine, sir – step out of the car and do the hokey-pokey."

"This Is Just Routine, Sir-Step Out of the Car and Do the Hokey-Pokey," cartoon by Jonny Hawkins. Copyright © Jonny Hawkins. Reproduced by permission of CartoonStock Ltd.

"if you drink and drive, you will be arrested, you will be prosecuted, and you could very well end up in a jail," effectively declaring a zero-tolerance policy. Not drunk driving, but any drinking and driving could be enough to at least subject you to delay at a checkpoint.

Checking the Wrong People

The problem with such policy is that it doesn't target the high BAC [blood alcohol concentration] drivers who cause the vast majority of alcohol-related traffic fatalities. Instead anyone could wind up being stopped and delayed—the caroling, eggnog-sipping, upright citizen who drinks moderately and responsibly before driving.

The deeply frustrating thing about these checkpoints is that there is a more effective, less intrusive alternative. A landmark National Highway Traffic Safety Administration study found that roving police patrols net nearly three times as many drunk drivers as roadblocks. That's because they are designed to find and pull over drivers who are actually impaired and thus a real hazard to themselves and others on the road.

Checkpoints, by contrast, simply pick up whoever wanders through, even if their blood alcohol concentration is well below the legal limit of .08 percent.

Meanwhile, the NHTSA report also found that roadblocks are not effective for catching "chronic drunk drivers," because they have learned how to avoid the publicized areas where roadblocks are set up—something innocent and responsible adults would never think of doing.

Checkpoints Hurt Innocent Drivers

The problem is that the 40 million Americans who drink responsibly before driving are being treated like the serious abusers whose actions lead to fatalities. In fact, numerous academic studies have shown that someone driving with a BAC at the legal limit is actually less "impaired" than someone driving with a hands-free cellphone.

Funding for roadblocks and increased pressure by federal authorities to promote "zero tolerance" policies has been ongoing for some time now. The result? Congress recently demanded an audit of the nation's drunk driving efforts after it found that there has been "no discernible progress" over the last six years.

Opponents of sobriety checkpoints believe they target the least dangerous drivers.

How Can Drunk Driving Be Prevented? 47

The shift away from focused attempts to catch drunk drivers to broader policies that target everyone who drinks and drives has yielded little result and caused a great deal of trouble for many innocent citizens.

States Without Checkpoints Have Fewer Deaths

When you divide the nation between those states that use roadblocks and those that don't, you find that every one of the 11 states that don't use roadblocks saw a drop in alcohol-related fatalities last year. In fact, of the 411 net fewer alcohol-related deaths in 2004 compared to 2003, 394 were realized by these 11 states.

Here's a modest proposal for this holiday season: End the intimidating sobriety field tests for thousands of responsible holiday revelers who simply enjoyed some eggnog. Targeted enforcement—not roadblocks designed to snare the wrong people—saves lives.

Though some of us may bristle at the intrusiveness of roadblocks, the real offense of this practice is that it is being done at the expense of far more effective tactics.

Considering the scarce resources we have to fight the deadly problem of drunk driving, we should all be outraged that PR campaigns are taking priority over actually getting drunk drivers off the roads.

> **EVALUATING THE AUTHORS' ARGUMENTS:**
>
> In this viewpoint the author makes the point that checkpoints inconvenience thousands of people who drink responsibly. Do you consider roadblocks or other kinds of security checkpoints to be an inconvenience or a necessary delay if they keep people safe? Explain your answer.

Viewpoint 3

Enforcing Underage Drinking Laws Can Reduce Drunk Driving

Insurance Institute for Highway Safety

"Studies of zero tolerance laws indicate they reduce crashes among drivers younger than 21."

In this viewpoint the Insurance Institute for Highway Safety (IIHS) argues that alcohol-related crashes among teens can be reduced by better enforcement of laws aimed at them. It explains that the crash risk for teens who drink and drive is much greater than for adults because teens are not experienced either with drinking or with driving. Therefore, more strictly enforcing laws that prohibit underage purchase of alcohol by teens and enforcing laws that create lower BAC [blood alchohol concentration] legal limits for teen drivers can reduce underage drinking and driving.

IIHS is a nonprofit organization dedicated to reducing crashes on the nation's highways.

"Q & A: Teenagers-Underage Drinking," Insurance Institute for Highway Safety, 2006. Copyright © 1996–2006, Insurance Institute for Highway Safety, Highway Lost Data Institute. Reproduced by permission.

AS YOU READ, CONSIDER THE FOLLOWING QUESTIONS:

1. Drivers age sixteen to twenty with BACs of from 0.05 to 0.08 are how many times more likely than sober teen drivers to be killed in single-car crashes, according to IIHS?
2. According to a study of twelve states cited by IIHS, what was the effect of passing zero tolerance laws on crashes involving drivers under age twenty-one?
3. Why, say the authors, is it difficult to enforce zero tolerance laws in some states?

Young drivers are less likely than adults to drive after drinking alcohol, but their crash risk is substantially higher when they do. This is especially true at low and moderate blood alcohol concentrations (BACs) and is thought to result from teenagers' relative inexperience with drinking, with driving, and with combining the two.

Teens and Drunk Driving

In 2004, 26 percent of 16–20-year-old passenger vehicle drivers fatally injured in crashes had high BACs (0.08 percent or higher). The percentage of fatally injured drivers with high BACs was much lower among females (14 percent) than among males (31 percent), and also was lower among 16–17-year-old drivers (15 percent) than among 18–19-year-old (27 percent) or 20-year-old (37 percent) drivers.

Drivers ages 16–20 with BACs of 0.05–0.08 percent are far more likely than sober teenage drivers to be killed in single-vehicle crashes—17 times more likely for males, 7 times more likely for females. At BACs of 0.08–0.10, fatality risks are even higher, 52 times for males, 15 times for females. . . .

Minimum alcohol purchasing age laws limit access to alcohol among teenagers. For a long time, the legal age for purchasing alcohol was 21 in most of the United States. Then in the 1960s and early 1970s, many states lowered their minimum purchasing ages to 18 or 19. However, states gradually restored higher minimum purchasing ages so that, by 1984, 23 states had minimum purchasing ages of 21, and federal legislation was enacted to withhold highway funds from the remaining 27 states if they did not follow suit. Since July 1988, all 50 states and the District of Columbia have had laws that require alcohol purchasers to be at least 21 years old.

All 50 states and the District of Columbia also have established lower blood alcohol thresholds that are illegal per se for drivers younger than 21. Federal legislation enacted in 1995 that allowed for the withholding of highway funds played a role in motivating states to pass such zero tolerance laws. Typically, these laws prohibit driving with a BAC of 0.02 percent or greater. . . .

Minimum Purchase Age and Zero Tolerance Laws Work

Yes. When minimum alcohol purchasing age laws were lowered in many states in the 1960s and early 1970s, Institute research indicated an increase in the number of drivers younger than 21 involved in nighttime fatal crashes. When a number of states restored higher

Drunk driving claims the lives of thousands of teenagers each year.

purchasing age laws as a result of this and other studies, Institute researchers in 1981 evaluated this development in 9 states, finding that nighttime fatal crashes among young drivers were reduced by 28 percent. A subsequent study in 26 states that raised minimum purchasing ages during 1975–84 estimated a 13 percent reduction in nighttime driver fatal crash involvement.

> **FAST FACT**
>
> According to a 2003 report in the *Journal of Studies on Alcohol*, each year more than 2 million college students aged eighteen to twenty-four drive after drinking. More than 3 million ride with drivers who have been drinking.

Studies of zero tolerance laws indicate they reduce crashes among drivers younger than 21. A study of 12 states that passed zero tolerance laws reported a 20 percent reduction in the proportion of fatal crashes that were single-vehicle nighttime events (crashes likely to involve alcohol impairment) among drivers ages 15–20. . . .

Trends in alcohol involvement in fatal crashes can be monitored through the National Highway Traffic Safety Administration's Fatality Analysis Reporting System, a census of virtually all fatal crashes in the United States. During the 1980s, the percentages of fatally injured drivers with high BACs (0.08 percent or higher) declined among drivers of all ages. Reductions among young drivers were greatest, in part because of changing minimum alcohol purchasing age laws. In 1982, fewer than half of the states had a minimum purchasing age of 21, and 49 percent of all fatally injured drivers younger than 21 had high BACs. This statistic declined dramatically as states adopted older purchasing age laws. By 1995, it had declined to 24 percent, the biggest improvement for any age group, but has edged higher since and was 26 percent in 2004. . . .

Better Enforcement Needed

States and communities need to make it more difficult for teenagers to purchase alcohol. During 1990–91, Institute researchers found that 19–20-year-olds could easily buy a six-pack of beer in Washington, D.C., and a New York City suburb. But in two New York counties where police recently had cracked down on underage alcohol

Checking identification for all alcohol purchases is one way to crack down on underage drinking and driving.

purchases, youths were less successful. In these studies, the underage purchasers generally were not even asked by sellers for proof of their ages. During 1994–95, Institute researchers surveyed high school and college students younger than 21 in New York and Pennsylvania about alcohol use and purchasing. Fifty-nine percent of college students and 28 percent of high school students in New York and 37 percent of college students and 14 percent of high school students in Pennsylvania reported they had used false identification to obtain alcohol. Clearly, stepping up enforcement of minimum alcohol purchasing age laws is needed to make them more effective.

Institute research has shown that the potential of zero tolerance laws has not been realized. Researchers found such laws difficult to enforce in some states because police must suspect that a young driver has a high BAC before administering an alcohol test for any measurable BAC. Institute surveys of young people in three states found limited knowledge about zero tolerance laws, and many of those who knew about the laws did not believe they often were enforced. Full enforcement of zero tolerance laws accompanied by publicity about the enforcement will be needed to increase effectiveness. Changes to the laws may encourage enforcement efforts.

> **EVALUATING THE AUTHORS' ARGUMENTS:**
>
> The IIHS claims that special laws targeting teens can reduce crashes from drunk driving. In your opinion, is it fair that laws for teen drivers should be different than laws for older drivers? If zero tolerance laws reduce alcohol-related accidents for teens, should these same laws be applied to drivers over age twenty-one? Why or why not?

Viewpoint 4

Chronic Drunk Drivers Require a Comprehensive Approach

National Commission Against Drunk Driving

"Because the majority of chronic drinking drivers are alcoholics, experts suggest ... combining treatment and legal sanctions."

Chronic drunk driving is difficult to prevent, according to the National Commission Against Drunk Driving (NCADD), because many of these drivers are alcoholics. NCADD says chronic drunk drivers avoid sobriety checkpoints. They are also more likely to drive illegally after their licenses have been suspended. Because of the complexity of the matter, a combination of approaches is needed to prevent convicted chronic drunk drivers from driving drunk again. These include using technology and treatment to dissuade drinkers from getting behind the wheel.

NCADD is a coalition of public and private organizations working to reduce drunk driving.

"What Research Says About Chronic Drinking and Ways to Apply This Research," National Commission Against Drunk Driving, Febuary 16, 2006.

AS YOU READ, CONSIDER THE FOLLOWING QUESTIONS:

1. How many people die each year as a result of individuals who continually drink and drive, according to the publisher?
2. What percentage of chronic drinking drivers continue to drink and drive after license suspension, according to estimates quoted by the pubisher?
3. How much money did Los Angeles save by using electronic mentoring instead of jail time for drunk drivers?

Approximately 10,000 people die and 250,000 people are injured each year as a result of individuals who continually drink and drive. In addition, chronic drinking drivers cost the economy $1.5 billion per year in enforcement and adjudication and $45 billion per year in property damage. The majority of chronic drinking drivers are white males between the ages of 21 and 34. More often than not, chronic drinking drivers are alcoholics or have a substance abuse problem. Assessment of DUI [driving under the influence] offenders in Maryland found that 70% were alcohol and/or drug dependent. A similar assessment of female DUI offenders in New York found that 43% could be diagnosed as alcohol dependent and 25% as alcohol abusers. Women diagnosed as alcohol dependent were also identified as having greater rates of psychological and social problems. Chronic drinking drivers also tend to be riskier drivers (e.g., more traffic violations) than the general driving population. Several studies have shown that chronic drinking drivers and risky drivers in general differ primarily with respect to levels of alcohol use and drinking problems, but not with respect to general patterns of driving behavior or personality characteristics. Also, chronic drunk drivers who are male, unmarried, and between the ages of 21 and 34 have a higher likelihood of dying in an alcohol-related crash. In addition, impaired drivers tend to use seat belts at half the rate of nonimpaired drivers, significantly increasing their risk of severe crash-related injury. Research on motor vehicle accident victims treated in emergency rooms indicates that over half may have an alcohol problem. Male victims should be screened, not just for positive BACs [blood alcohol concentrations], but for a history of prior treatment for trauma, motor vehicle accidents, and/or a history of DUI offenses, factors which are associated with the likelihood of having an alcohol problem.

While sobriety checkpoints have been found to be effective in deterring drunk drivers in general, there is some suggestion they may not be as effective for chronic drunk drivers, who may, if checkpoints operate in predictable locations, alter their driving behaviors to avoid them. Special DUI patrols and checkpoints which are assigned in an unpredictable manner may be more effective approaches to detecting and apprehending the chronic drunk driver.

License Suspensions

Research has identified several legal strategies that attempt to prevent chronic drinking drivers from [repeating offenses]. The most prevalent sanction levied against DUI offenders is license suspension. While the threat of license suspension has been an effective deterrent for the general population, chronic drinking drivers have demonstrated by their repeated violations that they are not as strongly affected by the loss of their license. The reason for this weaker deterrent effect may be

Top 10 Reasons Drivers Refrain from Drunk Driving

A 2005 MADD survey identified the top 10 reasons drivers are deterred from driving drunk:

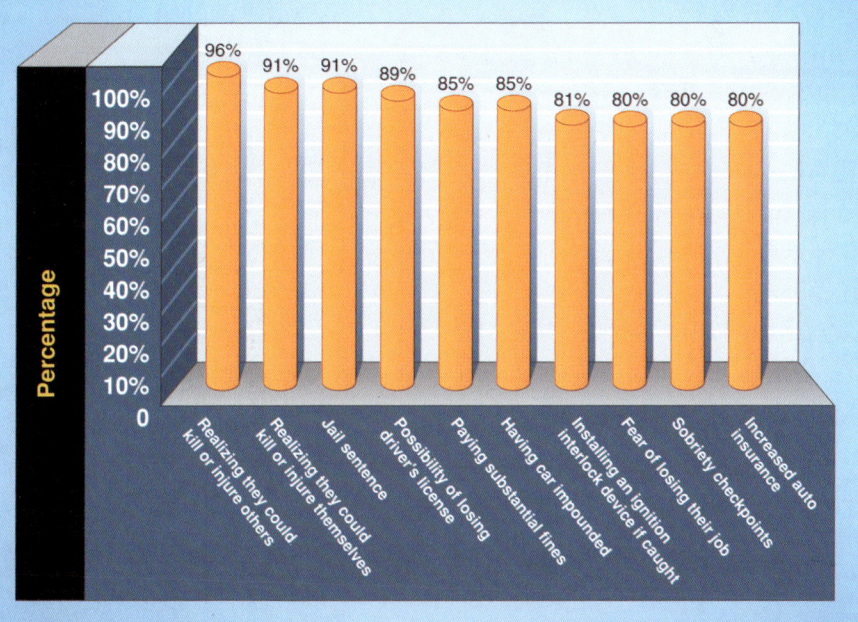

Reason	Percentage
Realizing they could kill or injure others	96%
Realizing they could kill or injure themselves	91%
Jail sentence	91%
Possibility of losing driver's license	89%
Paying substantial fines	85%
Having car impounded	85%
Installing an ignition interlock device if caught	81%
Fear of losing their job	80%
Sobriety checkpoints	80%
Increased auto insurance	80%

*Note: Answers do not equal 100% because respondents gave more than one answer.
Sources: Mothers Against Drunk Driving, 2005.

twofold. First, many chronic drinking drivers are alcoholic, which impairs their judgment and decision making skills. Secondly, in states where suspension is imposed as a penalty only after a criminal trial and conviction, the time between the arrest and license revocation is often long, and in some cases diversion programs allow the offenders to retain their licenses during the lengthy delay, both of which are associated with higher recidivism rates. Research has shown that to maximize the deterrent effects of a law the punishment must be perceived as certain, swift, and appropriately severe.

Persons caught driving while their licenses are suspended can be separated from their vehicles. This could be accomplished through the impoundment or immobilization of the vehicle, or the license

Officials demonstrate an ignition interlock device that prevents drivers from starting their vehicle if they fail a Breathalyzer test.

plates could be seized. This can occur administratively at the time of arrest. Research on the effectiveness of a vehicle immobilization law in Ohio revealed that the immobilization of vehicles driven by repeat drunk driving offenders produced significantly lower recidivism rates compared to offenders who did not receive this sanction. An evaluation of a license plate impoundment law in Minnesota found that DUI recidivism was cut in half. Alternatively, vehicles operated by drivers whose licences have been suspended could have their registrations revoked and special stickers placed over the vehicle registration tags to indicate registration status, providing probable cause for police officers to check the license status of the driver. This type of approach allows family members, who may be inconvenienced by stricter measures, to maintain use of the vehicle. An evaluation of such a sticker law in Oregon indicated that subsequent DUIs, crashes, and moving violations decreased, mainly because affected drivers drove more safely and less frequently.

It is estimated that up to 80% of chronic drinking drivers continue to drink and drive after license suspension, and the probability of being caught doing so is low. In addition, jail time, public service, and attendance at victim impact panels do little to stop chronic drinking drivers from drinking and driving after release. Long-term jail sentences would produce minimal crash reduction while overwhelming the correctional system with new inmates. There is virtually no difference in recidivism rates between those who receive jail time or public service only and those who do not. Due to the increasing cost of incarceration, the alcoholic tendencies exhibited by most chronic drinking drivers, and the high rearrest rates for chronic drinking drivers who receive traditional legal sanctions only, some jurisdictions have begun to use alternative sanctions, such as ignition interlock devices and electronic home monitoring, to deter recidivism.

Ignition Interlock Devices

Studies evaluating the effectiveness of ignition interlock devices have found that the rearrest rate for chronic drinking drivers is significantly reduced while the car is equipped with the device. A study of the effectiveness of interlock devices among a group of multiple DUI offenders in Maryland, who had successfully completed treatment

Some experts suggest mandated ignition interlock devices for chronic drunk drivers.

for alcohol problems, indicated that offenders assigned to the interlock program had recidivism rates during the sanction period which were one-third lower than that for offenders assigned to a control group. It should be noted that recidivism rates climb after the interlocks are removed, although one study in Canada found that recidivism rates were lower than for a comparison group of offenders, even 15 months after interlocks were removed. Some experts suggest that it may be necessary to mandate ignition interlock devices for an extended period of time for chronic drinking drivers. It is also suggested that offenders can be required to pay for the cost of the program, and, since interlock devices do not cure alcoholism, interlock programs should be combined with counseling. Offenders who violate the terms of the ignition interlock program or who are found tampering with the device could be placed on home arrest via electronic monitoring. This allows the offender to continue working and paying for the program. Also, electronic monitoring can be used as an alternative sanction in lieu of jail time. An electronic monitoring program in Los Angeles saved over $1 million in jail costs, and offenders who participated in the program had lower recidivism rates than offenders who were sentenced to jail. Intensive supervision probation, which requires more frequent contact with probation officers, has also been found to reduce recidivism when combined with other interventions.

Because the majority of chronic drinking drivers are alcoholics, experts suggest that combining treatment and legal sanctions will produce the largest benefit to traffic safety. A review of 215 studies of treatment for DUI offenders found that, compared to traditional legal sanctions, rehabilitation combined with license suspension was more effective in reducing recidivism. The most effective type of treatment included education, counseling, and follow-up supervision, such as probation or aftercare.

No single approach will solve the problem presented by chronic drinking drivers. The solution probably lies in a comprehensive approach consisting of legal sanctions in conjunction with mandated treatment, and in prevention activities.

> **EVALUATING THE AUTHORS' ARGUMENTS:**
>
> Consider the variety of suggestions made in this chapter for how to best prevent drunk driving. Rank each of the four viewpoints you read in the order of which you think is most convincing. Then, next to each one, explain why it appealed to you.

How Can Drunk Driving Be Prevented?

Chapter 3

How Should Laws Change to Discourage Drunk Driving?

A Maryland State Trooper holds a poster that expresses the states' attitude towards drunk drivers.

Viewpoint 1

A Higher Drinking Age Reduces Drunk Driving Fatalities

Robert Voas

"The [minimum drinking age of] 21 law has saved 23,733 lives since states began raising drinking ages in 1975."

In this viewpoint Robert Voas argues that lowering the drinking age would result in more highway accidents. Drinking is more dangerous for youths than for adults, he says, because youths are inexperienced with both alcohol and driving and are more likely to take risks. Voas says that European countries, which have lower drinking ages, also have a much higher binge drinking rate. New Zealand, he points out, recently lowered its drinking age and saw an increase of alcohol-related highway crashes. For these reasons, Voas concludes that the drinking age should be kept at twenty-one.

Voas is a research scientist at the Pacific Institute for Research and Evaluation.

Robert Voas, "There's No Benefit to Lowering the Drinking Age," *Christian Science Monitor*, January 12, 2006. Copyright © 2006 The Christian Science Monitor. Reproduced by permission.

A Higher Drinking Age Saves Lives

The NHTSA estimates that minimum-drinking-age laws save about 900 people per year, for a total of 23,733 lives saved since 1975.

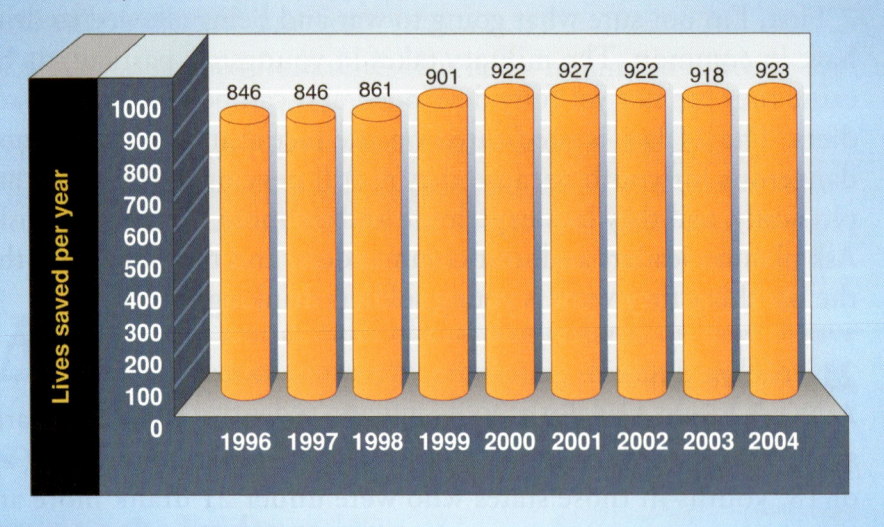

Year	Lives saved per year
1996	846
1997	846
1998	861
1999	901
2000	922
2001	927
2002	922
2003	918
2004	923

Sources: "Traffic Safety Facts," NHTSA's National Center for Statistics and Analysis, 2004.

continued to drink more as adults in their early 20s. In states where the drinking age was 21, teenagers drank less and continue to drink less through their early 20s.

And the minimum 21 law, by itself, has most certainly resulted in fewer accidents, because the decline occurred even when there was little enforcement and tougher penalties had not yet been enacted. According to the National Highway Traffic Safety Administration, the 21 law has saved 23,733 lives since states began raising drinking ages in 1975.

Europe's Problems

Do European countries really have fewer youth drinking problems? No, that's a myth. Compared to American youth, binge drinking rates among young people are higher in every European country except Turkey. Intoxication rates are higher in most countries; in Britain, Denmark, and Ireland they're more than twice the US level. Intoxication and binge drinking are directly linked to higher levels of alcohol-related problems, such as drinking and driving.

But, you drank when you were a kid, and you're OK. Thank goodness, because many kids aren't OK. An average of 11 American teens die each day from alcohol-related crashes. Underage drinking leads to increased teen pregnancy, violent crime, sexual assault, and huge costs to our communities. Among college students, it leads to 1,700 deaths, 500,000 injuries, 600,000 physical assaults, and 70,000 sexual assaults each year.

Recently, New Zealand lowered its drinking age, which gave researchers a good opportunity to study the impact. The result was predictable: The rate of alcohol-related crashes among young people rose significantly compared to older drivers.

Lowering the Drinking Age Is Dangerous

I've been studying drinking and driving for nearly 40 years and have been involved in public health and behavioral health for 53 years. Believe me when I say that lowering the drinking age would be very dangerous; it would benefit no one except those who profit from alcohol sales.

If bars and liquor stores can freely provide alcohol to teenagers, parents will be out of the loop when it comes to their children's decisions about drinking. Age 21 laws are designed to keep such decisions within the family where they belong. Our society, particularly our children and grandchildren, will be immeasurably better off if we not only leave the minimum drinking age law as it is, but enforce it better, too.

EVALUATING THE AUTHORS' ARGUMENTS:

In this viewpoint Robert Voas argues that the drinking age needs to remain at twenty-one. In the next viewpoint David J. Hanson argues in favor of lowering the drinking age. After carefully considering each person's arguments, explain which person you agree with, and why.

Viewpoint 2

The Drinking Age Should Be Lowered

David J. Hanson

> *"Lowering the drinking age would help send the important message that drinking is, in itself, not evidence of maturity."*

In the following viewpoint David Hanson conducts an interview with Ruth Engs, a professor at Indiana University who has proposed the drinking age be lowered. Engs reasons that setting the drinking age at twenty-one entices teens to abuse alcohol because it creates a "forbidden fruit" mentality around drinking. Waiting so long to officially introduce young people to alcohol causes them to use it responsibly, claims Engs. In addition, Engs believes it is unfair to make young people eligible for adult responsibilities such as serving in the military or voting but bar them from drinking. She concludes that the best way to teach young people to drink responsibly is to introduce them to alcohol at a younger age in controlled settings.

Ruth Engs is a professor of Applied Health Sciences at Indiana University in Bloomington. David Hanson is a professor of sociology at the State University of New York at Potsdam.

David J. Hanson, "The Drinking Age Should Be Lowered," interview with Dr. Ruth Engs, Alcohol Problems and Solutions, 2006. © Copyright 1997–2005 D. J. Hanson. All Rights Reserved for entire Web site. Reproduced by permission.

AS YOU READ, CONSIDER THE FOLLOWING QUESTIONS:

1. What age does Engs propose be set as the legal drinking age?
2. In what manner did people drink during eras of prohibition, according to Engs?
3. When were states required to raise the drinking age, as reported by Engs?

Dr. Hanson—
Dr. Engs, could you explain your proposal to lower the drinking age?

Dr. Engs—
I'd be glad to. I propose that the drinking age be lowered to about 18 or 19 and permit those of legal age to consume in socially controlled environments such as restaurants and official school and university functions. Currently, we prohibit 20-year-olds from sipping champagne at their own weddings! I also propose that individuals of any age be permitted to consume alcohol under the direct supervision of their parents in their own homes.

Dr. Hanson—
How would this be more effective than the 21 age laws?

Dr. Engs—
Although the legal purchase age is 21, a majority of young people under this age consume alcohol, and too many of them do so in an irresponsible manner. This is largely because drinking is seen by these youth as an enticing "forbidden fruit," a "badge of rebellion against authority," and a symbol of adulthood. Our nation has twice tried prohibition, first at the state level in the 1850's and at the national level beginning in 1920. These efforts to prevent drinking were unenforceable and created serious social problems such as widespread disrespect for law, the growth of organized crime, and the development of immoderate consumption patterns.

> **FAST FACT**
>
> Fifty-two percent of male college students and 35 percent of female college students binge drink occasionally or regularly, according to the University of Michigan Health System.

Supporters of a reduced drinking age believe that if teenagers were exposed to alcohol earlier, they would handle it with sophistication and intelligence.

The flaunting of the current age-specific prohibition is readily apparent among young people who, since the increase in the minimum legal drinking age, have tended to drink in a more abusive manner than do those of legal age. This, of course, is exactly what happened in the general public during national Prohibition.

A Counterproductive Drinking Age
Dr. Hanson—
So raising the legal drinking age has made things worse?
Dr. Engs—
Yes. Like national Prohibition, it has been counter-productive. Raising the drinking age was much worse than doing nothing.

Dr. Hanson—

But hasn't drinking been going down among young people?

Dr. Engs—

Yes, the proportion of the American population who drink (including young people) has been going down since about 1980. That was long before the states were required to raise the drinking age in 1987. And of course legislation wouldn't have limited consumption among those aged 21 or older.

On the other hand, while fewer young people are drinking and their average consumption levels have been dropping (along with that of the general population), more younger people tend to drink abusively when they do consume. This change occurred after the increase in the drinking age.

The Drinking Age Promotes Abuse

Dr. Hanson—

So, it's a little like what happened during national Prohibition?

Dr. Engs—

Exactly. Prohibition tended to destroy moderation and instead promoted great excess and abusive drinking. People tended to gulp alcohol in large quantities on those occasions when they could obtain it. The notorious speakeasies didn't exist before prohibition, when people could drink legally and leisurely. What we currently have is age-specific prohibition and young people are forced to create their own "speakeasies" in dorm rooms and other secret locations where they, too, must gulp their alcohol in the absence of moderating social control.

Dr. Hanson—

You're saying that simply lowering the drinking age would solve the problem of drinking abuse among young people?

Dr. Engs—

Unfortunately, it wouldn't solve the problem. However, it would be an important step in the right direction.

The experience of many societies and groups demonstrates that drinking problems are reduced when young people learn at home from their parents how to drink in a moderate and responsible manner. As parents we need to be good role models in what we say and do.

Drinking Ages in Europe

Drinking Age:
- 14 yrs. old
- 16 yrs. old
- 18 yrs. old
- No Minimum

Source: James Gilden, "Alcohol Figures into Some Young Americans' European Plans," *Los Angeles Times*, May 15, 2005.

And lowering the drinking age would help send the important message that drinking is, in itself, not evidence of maturity . . . that responsible consumption for those who choose to drink is evidence of maturity.

Teach Young People to Drink Responsibly

We need to reinforce the norm of moderation by making it clear that the abuse of alcohol is completely unacceptable by anyone. This would help stress that it is not drinking that is the problem but rather drinking abusively that is the problem.

Dr. Hanson—
These ideas may sound great, but would they really work?

Dr. Engs—

These proposals are not based on speculation but on the proven example set by many societies and groups around the world that have long used alcohol extensively with very few problems.

On the other hand, our current prohibition directed against the consumption of alcohol by young people (who can marry, serve in the military, vote, enter into legal contracts, and shoulder adult responsibilities) is clearly not working. We need to abandon this failed and demeaning folly and replace it with a proven, realistic, and successful approach to reducing drinking problems.

> **EVALUATING THE AUTHORS' ARGUMENTS:**
>
> In this viewpoint Ruth Engs reasons that if teenagers are old enough to vote and to serve in the military, they are old enough to be allowed to drink. What do you think? At what age do you think it is appropriate to be allowed to vote, serve, and drink? Should they be allowed at the same age, or are different activities better suited for different ages? Explain your reasoning.

Viewpoint 3

Lower Blood Alcohol Content Limits Reduce Drunk Driving

Mark Asbridge, Robert E. Mann, Rosely Flam-Zalcman, and Gina Stoduto

"The introduction of legal [0.08%] BAC limits has had a long-term impact on alcohol-related fatalities."

In the following viewpoint Gina Stoduto presents the results of a study analyzing the effect of Canada's 1969 Breathalyzer Law that made 0.08 percent blood alcohol concentration (BAC) the legal level for drunk driving. Controlling for other factors, the author concludes that the 0.08 percent BAC law significantly reduced drunk driving fatalities. She argues the law also may have worked to educate Canadians not to drink and drive.

The authors are experts on drunk driving and authors of *Existing Remedial Programs for Convicted Drinking Drivers in Canada*.

Mark Asbridge, Robert E. Mann, Rosely Flam-Zalcman, and Gina Stoduto, "The Criminalization of Impaired Driving in Canada: Assessing the Deterrent Impact of Canada's First Per Se Law," in *Journal of Studies on Alcohol*, July 1, 2004, pp. 450–59. Reproduced by permission.

AS YOU READ, CONSIDER THE FOLLOWING QUESTIONS:

1. How much, according to the author, did the Breathalyzer Law reduce drunk driving fatalities between 1969 and 1996?
2. What effect did the Breathalyzer law have on Canadian attitudes about drinking and driving?
3. What does the word "deterrent" mean in the context of the viewpoint?

The goal of this article is to assess the effectiveness of Canada's first per se law criminalizing driving with a blood alcohol concentration of over 0.08%, the Breathalyser Law introduced in 1969, in reducing drinking-driver-related fatalities. We also examine the long-term deterrent effect of this law on driver fatality rates. In the analyses we include such potentially confounding influences on drinking-driver fatality rates as the founding of Mothers Against Drunk Driving (MADD), Canada; the introduction of Ontario's mandatory seatbelt law; per capita alcohol consumption; the unemployment rate; vehicles registered per capita; and precipitation rates. . . .

.08% BAC Reduced Fatalities

On December 1, 1969, Canada introduced its first per se law, the Breathalyser legislation, criminalizing impaired driving over a BAC [blood alcohol concentration] limit. The 1969 Breathalyser legislation (Sections 234, 235, 236) was adapted, in part, from the 1921 amendment to the Canadian Criminal Code and from the British Road Safety Act of 1967. . . . The law made it illegal, per se, to drive with more than 80 mg of alcohol in 100 milliliters of blood and made it mandatory for drivers to take a breath test via a breath analyzer device when requested by the police. . . . Individuals who tested over the legal limit or refused to provide a breath sample would be charged with a criminal code offense—with penalties ranging from a fine and driving prohibition for a first offense to up to 2 years imprisonment for third and subsequent offenses. . . .

Reducing Fatalities Without Infringing on Rights

The introduction of the Breathalyser Law leads to a significant decrease in drinking-driver fatalities. Based on the estimated attributable

"Well, according to the Breathalyzer, you have been drinking—from the toilet."

"Well, Acording to the Breathalyzer...," cartoon by Mike Baldwin. Reproduced by permission.

fraction for the intervention measure, the introduction of the Breathalyser Law is associated with an 18% reduction in the proportion of drinking-driver fatalities in Ontario in the period between 1969 and 1996....

The Breathalyser legislation led to an observed decline in drunk-driver fatalities; however, a similar effect was not demonstrated with respect to nondrinking-driver fatalities. The Breathalyser Law effect on nondrinking-driver fatalities was not measurable and was dwarfed by the robust effects of the enactment of MADD, Canada, and OMSL. On the basis of the driver fatality data, therefore, Canada's per se law represents an effective deterrent for drunk driving, with little or no impact on fatalities that do not involve drinking drivers. . . .

BAC Limits Work

The question of interest is whether the enactment of the 1969 Breathalyser legislation in Canada produced a decrease in drinking-driver fatalities. Previous evaluations demonstrated that the Breathalyser Law produced a marginal decrease in fatalities; however, this decrease continued for only a short period of time, and fatalities eventually returned to prelaw levels in the months following passage of the law. The current analysis confirms that the 1969 Breathalyser Law was associated with a decline in drinking-driver fatalities. Controlling for other explanatory measures, drinking-driver fatalities decreased approximately 18% in the period 1969–1996 compared to the period 1962–1968. The observed decline in drinking-driver fatalities is consistent with previous research on per se laws. This research extends previous findings in that we observe an enduring reduction in drinking-driving fatalities in the 27 years following the enactment of Canada's Breathalyser Law, whereas the early research

Blood Alcohol Content and Impairment

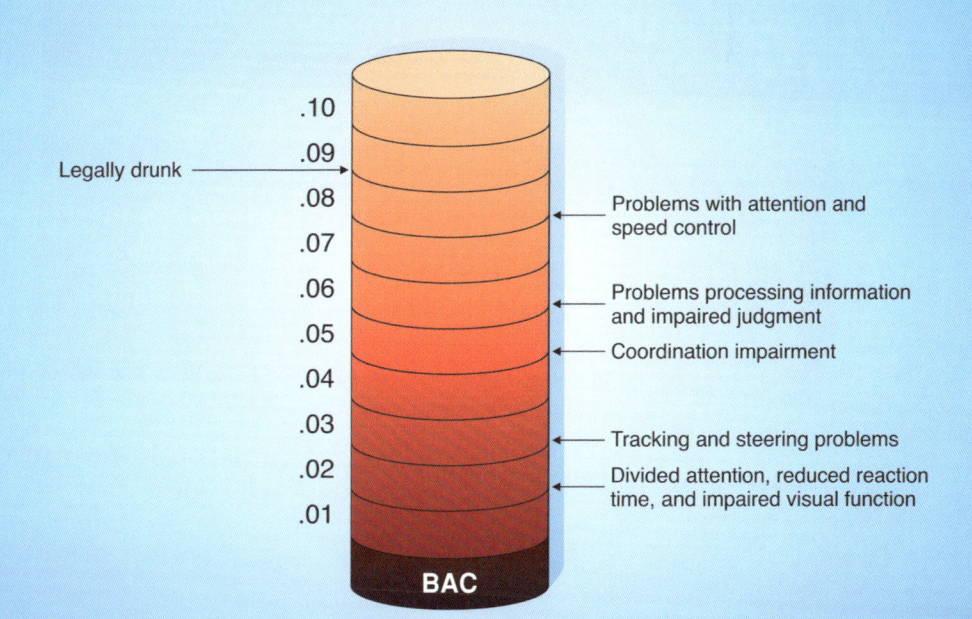

BAC	Effect
.10	
.09	Legally drunk
.08	Problems with attention and speed control
.07	
.06	Problems processing information and impaired judgment
.05	Coordination impairment
.04	
.03	Tracking and steering problems
.02	Divided attention, reduced reaction time, and impaired visual function
.01	

Source: National Highway Traffic Safety Administration (NHTSA).

found only short-term reductions in fatalities. Our finding . . . demonstrates that the introduction of legal BAC limits has had a long-term impact on alcohol-related fatalities. . . .

Changing Public Thinking

The intended consequence of the Canadian Breathalyser Law was a reduction in drunk-driving incidents and, subsequently, a reduction in impaired collisions and fatalities. Judged by the available evidence, the Breathalyser Law has accomplished this task, modestly in the first couple of years and more robustly when examined over the long term.

This study also points to an unintended consequence of the Breathalyser legislation—the change in social norms regarding impaired driving. Ross (1984) speculated that legal efforts to control impaired driving, while not immediately effective, produced long-term behavior change through shifting social norms. In other words, law also acts to educate and transform social behavior while providing support for the emergence of other institutional reforms concerning drinking and driving. It may be that the Breathalyser Law, while producing an immediate but modest impact on fatalities in the early 1970s, helped to transform public thinking about impaired driving in Canada.

> **EVALUATING THE AUTHORS' ARGUMENTS:**
>
> This viewpoint claims that the 0.08 percent BAC level reduces drunk driving fatalities. The author of the next viewpoint argues that such a low level is unfair to motorists who pose no risk to others. After considering the points made by both authors, what do you think the BAC limit should be?

Viewpoint 4

Blood Alcohol Content Limits Should Be Higher

National Motorists Association

"By targeting higher BAC operators and repeat offenders, the state can focus its enforcement and treatment efforts on truly dangerous drivers."

In the following viewpoint by the National Motorists Association (NMA), the authors argue that .08 percent blood alcohol concentration (BAC) level standards are too low and unfairly penalize motorists who pose no risk to others. Most serious accidents occur when drivers have a BAC of 0.15 percent or higher, the authors claim —therefore, targeting people who have a BAC of 0.08 percent will bring in many harmless people who have just had a drink or so. A 0.12 percent BAC is more reasonable, the authors conclude, and would allow law enforcement to focus on dangerous hardcore drunk drivers.

NMA claims to advocate, represent, and promote the interests of North American motorists.

AS YOU READ, CONSIDER THE FOLLOWING QUESTIONS:

1. What punishments might unfairly be meted out to what the NMA considers to be responsible, social drinkers?

National Motorists Association "NMA Position on Drunk Driving," www.Motorists.org, 2006. Copyright © National Motorists Association. All rights reserved. Reproduced by permission.

2. What BAC level, according to the authors, is involved in the average DWI arrest?
3. According to NMA, how does the 0.08 percent BAC limit affect people who might patronize eating and drinking establishments, community festivals, and company picnics?

Historically, the BAC for automatic categorization as "drunk driving" was .15%. This was, and is, the level where impairment is usually readily discernable. Most fatal and serious accidents involving alcohol continue to reflect .15% or higher BACs. . . .

Lowered BAC levels serve to intimidate casual and social drinkers and give the police unbridled discretion to test and arrest almost anyone who has been drinking. Meanwhile, true drunk drivers floating along with .25% BACs continue to wreak havoc on the highways. A law enforcement officer cannot be looking for swerving, careening drunks if he is tied up with the processing of some miscreant who had four beers at the church picnic and blew a .09% BAC, after a traffic stop for a burned out license plate bulb. . . .

Penalties Should Be Reasonable

The notion that severe penalties can deter drunk drivers has some validity. However, that deterrence often lasts no longer than the length of the punishment. The individuals who personify the public's image of a drunk driver are not typically swayed by "get tough" laws. However, a responsible, social drinker, apprehended in a "sobriety checkpoint," could well find himself facing license revocation, jail time, five years of horrendous insurance surcharges, and possibly the loss of his job. It happens every single day to people who have hurt no one and who are not a threat to anyone's well-being.

Draconian penalties are promoted by persons who are primarily interested in an overall assault on the use of alcohol, or are motivated by revenge. Developing solutions to the complicated problem of drunk driving and the resulting tragedies is not one of their priorities. . . .

Low BAC Standards Cause Other Harms

A discussion of the unintended and negative consequences of the current catalog of anti-DWI laws is seldom found in the print or electronic media, nor has there been a concerted effort on the part of government or private organizations to research and quantify these effects. As a result, certain of the following remarks are anecdotal rather than being based on actual research results. . . .

Persons who might otherwise assume responsibility for an accident or render assistance to accident victims are intimidated by the possibility of being found guilty of "drunk driving," even if they had drunk very little and were not directly involved in causing the accident. Consequently, they do not stop or render assistance. . . .

We have read of threefold increases in drivers attempting to outrun police. This increase corresponds with the ratcheting downward

A police officer administers a Breathalyzer test to a suspected drunk driver. Breathalyzer tests measure the level of alcohol in the bloodstream.

of legal BACs and the ratcheting upward of DWI penalties. It has been reported in more than one source that one in four high speed pursuits results in a serious accident, often involving innocent bystanders. . . .

Scaring the Public

For fear of being reported to police or being charged at the scene of an accident for DWI, people are deliberately leaving an accident scene, injured, and not reporting for treatment until there is no likelihood that they could be charged with DWI. This runs counter to the well-proven practice that immediate injury treatment is the most effective and the most likely to prevent loss of life. . . .

The segment of the population most affected, and most intimidated by the current avalanche of DWI laws is not the alcoholic or hardcore drinking crowd. It is that group of people who might patronize eating and drinking establishments, community festivals, company picnics, and related hospitality businesses, and who con-

Some argue that low blood alcohol concentration laws unfairly penalize occasional social drinkers who pose little threat to other drivers.

duct themselves in a responsible manner. The difference is, with .08% BACs and job threatening sanctions, they are now afraid to participate in this type of social activity with friends and relatives.

The businesses and organizations that cater to and sponsor these activities suffer accordingly in lost income and lost support.

Target Hardcore Drunk Drivers

Intimidating, apprehending, adjudicating, and jailing persons who are not serious hardcore offenders takes valuable resources away from locating, stopping, and treating the persons who are most likely to cause a DWI-related accident. The system can only process and accommodate so many people. The choice is to focus on those who are causing the problem, or severely punish the general population that crosses an arbitrary BAC threshold. . . .

The "one size fits all" and "hang 'em from the highest tree" mentality that dominates current anti-DWI strategies does not fairly accommodate the diversity of circumstances involved with DWI convictions. A high risk, accident-prone, repeat offender may view a DWI conviction as one of life's little inconveniences and a chance to live off the county for 30 days. Conversely, a well-educated, successful employee and family man might lose his job, future employment opportunities, and reputation for a one-time technical violation of a BAC standard based on politics and platitudes. . . .

The standard retort to any of the aforementioned concerns is "don't drink and drive and you won't suffer these consequences." This is comparable to saying "if you don't want to get speeding tickets, don't drive over the speed limit."

Most People Act Responsibly

Any law or regulation aimed at human activity must have an element of reasonableness. It must recognize that there are always competing motivations that dictate human behavior.

Most people drive to reach a destination. The purpose of that destination may be work, family responsibilities, maintenance tasks, socializing, or recreation.

In our society (as in most societies), the vast majority of the adult population consumes beverages containing alcohol. If this is at the destination end of their trip, they will inevitably be returning with some amount of alcohol in their systems. In modest amounts, this rarely causes a problem or safety risk to others. Most people recognize this and act accordingly, in a responsible manner.

A zero tolerance approach to drinking and driving will not work. Moreover, it will expose motorists to a rash of officially sanctioned abuses that will exceed any of those we currently endure.

BAC Should Not Determine Guilt

Discernable impairment need not be BAC dependent. Different people experience different levels of impairment at the same BAC levels. If a person's driving indicates impairment (e.g., erratic maneuvers or speeds, or running into fixed objects) and they have alcohol in their systems, they should be a candidate for a DWI citation.

If a single standard BAC is to be established as the automatic threshold for a DWI citation, it should be high enough to reflect discernable impairment among the general population. An appropriate and enforceable BAC of .12% would represent a reasonable standard.

> **FAST FACT**
>
> A driver with a 0.15 percent BAC is 385 times more likely to be involved in a fatal crash than a driver with a BAC of zero, according to the National Hardcore Drunk Driver Project.

Please note that we are not saying a 12% BAC is necessary for a DWI conviction. Rather, that for an automatic DWI conviction that does not involve or require discernable impairment the BAC must be at least .12%. Given that the average DWI arrest involves a BAC of 15% to .17% (regardless of the legal BAC), a .12% BAC remains well below the typical level for DWI arrests. It is also a level of intoxication that most persons will recognize as representing a degree of impairment.

A Higher BAC Gets to the Heart of the Problem

Penalties and punishment for DWI convictions should reflect the degree of intoxication and the severity of the circumstance. A person charged with having a .25% BAC should be assessed a greater penalty than someone charged with a .12% BAC. Furthermore, if an intoxicated driver causes property damage or personal injury, the

"The Bloke Buying You All the Pints? That's Charlie, The Local Taxi Driver…," cartoon by Sam Smith. Copyright © Sam Smith. Reproduced by permission of CartoonStock, Ltd., www.CartoonStock.com.

penalties should reflect those losses and be paid to the victims, not the state.

By targeting higher BAC operators and repeat offenders, the state can focus its enforcement and treatment efforts on truly dangerous drivers, the small percentage of true drunk drivers that menace our streets, roads, and highways.

EVALUATING THE AUTHORS' ARGUMENTS:

The NMA bases its argument for raising blood alcohol content levels on the idea that zero tolerance laws, laws that strictly punish even the slightest infraction, are inappropriate. What do you think? Is zero tolerance a good approach for punishing drunk drivers, or does such an approach punish the people who do not most deserve it? Explain your reasoning.

Viewpoint 5

Mandatory Ignition Interlock Laws Will Reduce Drunk Driving

"An interlock device is like a mechanical probation officer on duty and monitoring DWI offenders 24 hours per day and seven days per week."

Haya el Nasser

In the following viewpoint Haya el Nasser discusses how ignition interlock devices are used to prevent repeat drunk driving. Forty-three states, she explains, have the option of making convicted drunk drivers use ignition interlocks, which require a driver to breathe into a machine in their car before allowing the car's ignition to be started. El Nasser notes that parents worried about teen driving habits can voluntarily install the devices. Devices requiring random breath samples while the person is driving can also prevent a drunk person from getting a sober person to start their car for them, she argues.

El Nasser is a reporter for *USA Today*, from which this viewpoint was taken.

Haya el Nasser, "States Turn on to Idea of Ignition Locks," *USA Today*, June 23, 2005, copyright 2005, USA Today. Reproduced by permission.

AS YOU READ, CONSIDER THE FOLLOWING QUESTIONS:

1. About how many ignition interlocks are in use in the United States, according to sources quoted by the author?
2. What state has the highest per capita number of ignition interlocks on cars?
3. How much do interlock devices cost per year, as reported by El Nasser?

More convicted drunken drivers may have to blow into devices that won't let them start their cars if they're intoxicated now that several states are embracing tougher penalties.

New Mexico [in June of 2005] became the first state to require "ignition interlock" systems for first-time offenders. The devices, which act as breath-alcohol analyzers that control a car's ignition, will be on their cars for one year. Drivers with four or more DWI convictions are required to drive with the interlocks for the rest of their lives.

The devices cost the offenders about $1,000 a year.

Until now, they were required only for repeat offenders and for a maximum of a year.

"This is the first time it's been so broad," Jonathan Adkins, communications director for the Governors Highway Safety Association, says of the New Mexico law. "States realize we haven't won the drunken driving battle yet."

At the same time, the Senate version of a federal highway spending bill before Congress threatens to withhold about $600 million in highway construction and maintenance funds if states don't subject high-risk offenders to stiffer sanctions, including ignition interlocks and license suspensions.

Excellent Tool

Mothers Against Drunk Driving says 17,000 people are killed and a half-million injured in alcohol-related crashes every year. Only 18 states have mandatory ignition interlock laws, according to MADD President Wendy Hamilton.

"They have to play a bigger role," she says about the devices. "They're an excellent tool and should be used for higher-risk drivers."

"Would you mind blowing into this bag sir?"

"Would You Mind Blowing into this Bag Sir?" Cartoon by Kes. Copyright © Kes. Reproduced by permission of CartoonStock, Ltd., www.CartoonStock.com.

High-risk drivers include repeat offenders and those convicted of driving with a blood-alcohol level of 0.15% or higher. By August [2005], when a Minnesota law goes into effect, the legal limit in every state will be 0.08%.

Forty-three states and the District of Columbia have the option to make convicted drunken drivers use interlocks, MADD says. More are making them mandatory, applying the sentence to all offenders or lengthening the penalty:

- This month [June 2005], Florida Gov. Jeb Bush signed a bill that allows the state to require the device without a court order.
- [In 2004], Washington state began requiring interlocks for first-time offenders with a blood-alcohol level of 0.15% or higher.
- New York Assemblyman Felix Ortiz, who spearheaded legislation that bans hands-on use of cell phones while driving in his

state, introduced a bill that would require interlocks on all new cars. A similar measure failed in New Mexico [in 2004], but others are being proposed in New Jersey, Connecticut and Washington state.

Increasing Use

About 80,000 interlocks are used in the USA, according to Lamar Ball, chief executive of Smart Start Inc., a manufacturer in Irving, Texas.

"I would expect that to more than double in the next five years," he says. His business is growing 30% a year.

Interlocks also can be installed voluntarily by parents who worry about their teenage children's driving habits. The system keeps a log of failed attempts to turn on the ignition.

Some drivers have tried to bypass the system by starting the car when sober and drinking while the engine is running. Others have used air compressor hoses. The devices now require random breath samples while the person is driving. They have only a few minutes to comply.

> **FAST FACT**
> The International Council on Alcohol, Drugs, and Traffic Safety says that use of interlock ignition programs reduces repeat drunk driving by up to 95 percent as long as the device remains on the car.

Amy Berning, research psychologist at the National Highway Transportation Safety Administration, says interlocks are "extremely effective" when they're on a car. "The concern is when the devices come off the vehicle, the recidivism starts to go back up."

Mechanical Probation Officer

New Mexico, which ranks sixth in the nation in the rate of alcohol-related car fatalities, is becoming one of the toughest enforcers. There are 3,000 interlocks on cars in the state, the highest per capita of any state.

In 2003, 198 of New Mexico's 439 traffic fatalities were alcohol-related, according to the most recent government data. It was the first time since 1998 that the state's alcohol-related fatalities fell below 200.

Fighting drunken driving is one of Gov. Bill Richardson's signature issues. He has appointed DWI Czar Rachel O'Connor and several task forces to tackle the problem of repeat offenders and set up drunken-driving checkpoints statewide.

"An interlock device is like a mechanical probation officer on duty and monitoring DWI offenders 24 hours per day and seven days per week," Richardson says. "It's a wonderful device. It's going to dramatically curb DWI in New Mexico."

> **EVALUATING THE AUTHORS' ARGUMENTS:**
>
> The author of this viewpoint discusses how ignition interlock technology can help reduce drunk driving by forcing drivers to submit to a Breathalyzer test in their own car. She notes that only eighteen states have mandatory ignition interlock laws, however. Given the other evidence the author presents for why ignition interlock laws can reduce drunk driving, why do you think only eighteen states have made such laws mandatory? Explain your ideas.

Viewpoint 6

Interlock Ignition Programs Are Not Always Effective at Reducing Drunk Driving

David J. DeYoung, Helen N. Tashima, and Scott V. Masten

"Much of California's interlock program is ineffective in reducing DUI recidivism."

In the following viewpoint David J. DeYoung, Helen N. Tashima, and Scott V. Masten present the results of a study of California's ignition interlock program that show that such devices are not always effective at reducing drunk driving. The authors agree that interlock ignition devices (IID) may reduce repeat DUIs for some offenders if the devices are actually installed. But they argue that orders to install IIDs are not often followed by offenders. Furthermore, drivers who install IIDs tend to have a higher risk of crashes than drivers who do not install IIDs, and the

David J. DeYoung, Helen N. Tashima and Scott V. Masten, "An Evaluation of the Effectiveness of Ignition Interlock in California: Report to the Legislature of the State of California," Sacramento, CA: State of California, Department of Motor Vehicles, 2004. © 2004 State of California. Reproduced by permission.

device does not prevent them from getting into crashes. For these reasons, the authors are wary of depending too much on ignition interlock devices to reduce drunk driving.

The authors wrote this report for the Research and Development Branch of the California Department of Motor Vehicles.

AS YOU READ, CONSIDER THE FOLLOWING QUESTIONS:
1. What does the word "brevity" mean in the context of the viewpoint?
2. Which category of DUI offenders are judges required by California law to order to install an IID?
3. How long has California's ignition interlock program run, as reported by the authors?

California's ignition interlock laws prescribe and authorize the use of IIDs for different offenders in different situations, so that California's ignition interlock program is really several different programs. Two examples are that (1) judges are required to order IIDs for DWS*-DUI offenders, and (2) multiple DUI offenders can choose to end their license suspension or revocation term early by installing an IID. Because of this, the outcome evaluation is comprised of six different studies, each of which assesses the effectiveness of IIDs for different types of offenders, with the devices used in a specific context. Taken together, these six studies provide a comprehensive picture of the effectiveness of IIDs as a traffic safety countermeasure in California. . . .

The effectiveness of ignition interlock was assessed by comparing the rates of subsequent *DUI convictions* and *crashes* between the IID and comparison groups. A third outcome measure, subsequent DUI incidents, which represents DUI convictions, alcohol-related crashes, and Administrative Per Se (APS) actions, was also examined. The results based on DUI incidents were very similar to those for DUI convictions for 4 of the 6 studies, and for the sake of

* DWS = Driving While Suspended

brevity, the results for DUI incidents are only discussed for the two studies where they differed from those for DUI convictions....

Orders to Install IIDs Have Little Effect

The results from this study are mixed. They show that IIDs can be effective in reducing DUI recidivism, but not in all situations or for all offenders. When DUI recidivism is examined, the results indicate that IIDs are effective in reducing subsequent DUI convictions when they are actually installed on offenders' vehicles, but that requiring judges to order offenders to install interlock devices and/or restrict offenders to driving IID-equipped vehicles generally has little effect. To the extent that most other studies of interlock have

Ignition interlock devices, such as the one pictured, prevent a car from being started by a drunk driver. But it is unclear whether such devices reduce drunk driving.

A ranger examines an overturned van following a drunk-driving accident. In spite of many laws to reduce its incidence, drunk driving remains a problem in the United States.

focused on situations where the devices are actually installed, the findings from this study are in accord with prior research.

Thus, it could be said that IIDs are efficacious, but not necessarily effective, or that the devices themselves can work, but that programs utilizing them are more problematic. This is certainly the case in California, where after almost two decades of experience with interlocks, a truly effective program has yet to be developed. The findings from the process evaluation of California's program show that judges do not order most DWS-DUI offenders to install an IID, as required by law, and that only a minority of those who do receive an order comply and actually install a device. Given this, the findings from the current study that much of California's interlock program is ineffective in reducing DUI recidivism are not surprising.

Offenders Who Install IIDs Get into More Accidents

The effectiveness of IIDs can also be measured by examining their effects on crashes. Crashes could be considered an important, albeit unintended, effect of California's program. Interestingly, the results of this study showed that offenders who received an interlock order/restriction had a *lower* risk of crashes than offenders who did not receive an order, even though there was no difference between the groups on DUI recidivism. The explanation for these findings is not completely clear, although it seems likely that the reduction in crashes is due to a change in offenders' driving, similar to what happens when a license suspension order is issued. Studies have shown that suspended drivers drive less often and more carefully, to avoid detection by law enforcement. The situation is similar with DWS-DUI/DUI offenders who have been ordered by the court to install an IID; most such offenders do not comply, and they may drive more carefully and less frequently, in order to avoid being apprehended for violating a court order.

The relationship between IDs and crashes changes when crashes are examined for offenders who installed an interlock device. Surprisingly, the two analyses that examined this both showed that the risk of crashes was *higher* for offenders installing an interlock. Thus, even though installing an IID is associated with a reduction in DUI recidivism, it is also linked with an increase in crash risk, so that the overall traffic safety effect of IIDs are mixed, even when installed. With the exception of a study of Oregon's interlock program, which also found that IIDs were associated with an increase in crashes, prior research on IIDs has generally not examined the devices' effect on crashes, so the findings of this study are somewhat unique, and in need of replication. One possible explanation for the findings here is that drivers installing IIDs generally obtain restricted driver licenses, and so may drive more and thus have more exposure than drivers not installing a device, many of whom remain suspended.

IID Orders Have No Effect on First-Time Offenders

This study also examined whether IIDs are more effective with DWS-DUI or DUI drivers. One analysis clearly demonstrated that IIDs are linked with reduced DUI recidivism for DWS-DUI offenders who installed an interlock device, and the study examining repeat DUI offenders receiving an IID order/restriction showed that such an order or restriction was linked with a reduced risk of DUI recidivism and crashes. One group for whom the devices seem to have little effect is first DUI offenders; first offenders ordered to install a device/receiving an interlock restriction had the same risk of subsequent crash and DUI conviction as first offenders not receiving an order/restriction. All first offenders in the current study had elevated BAC levels, with an average BAC of .20%, and could be considered high risk. . . .

The results of this study are mixed and somewhat complex regarding the effectiveness of IIDs in California. IIDs are not the "silver bullet" that will solve the DUI problem.

EVALUATING THE AUTHORS' ARGUMENTS:

Consider the variety of suggestions made in this chapter for how laws might be changed to discourage drunk driving. Rank each of the six viewpoints you read in the order of which you think is most convincing. Then, next to each one, explain why it appealed to you.

Facts About Drunk Driving

Drunk Driving in the United States
- According to the State of Illinois, nearly two out of every five Americans will be involved in an alcohol-related traffic crash in their lifetime.
- States with the highest rates of fatal alcohol-related crashes are: Alaska (52.8 percent), Texas (49.8 percent), North Dakota (47.8 percent), Massachusetts (47.4 percent), and Arizona (45.5 percent).
- States with the lowest rates of fatal alcohol-related crashes are: Utah (20.6 percent), New York (27.4 percent), Arkansas (29.2 percent), Kansas (29.5 percent), Wyoming (31.5 percent).
- The National Highway Traffic Safety Administration (NHTSA) recorded 16,694 alcohol-related fatalities in 2004—39 percent of the total traffic fatalities for the year.
- Traffic fatalities in alcohol-related crashes fell by 2.4 percent, from 17,105 in 2003 to 16,694 in 2004.

According to the U.S. Department of Transportation:
- There is an alcohol-related traffic fatality every thirty minutes, and an alcohol-related traffic injury every two minutes.
- About 1.5 million drivers are arrested each year for driving under the influence of alcohol or narcotics.
- Motor vehicle crashes are the leading cause of death for Americans from age three to thirty-three.
- There is about one alcohol- or narcotics-related driving arrest for every 137 licensed drivers in the United States.
- About 30 percent of all Americans will be involved in an alcohol-related crash at some point in their lives.

Teens and Drunk Driving

- According to the State of Illinois, although sixteen- to twenty-four-year-olds comprise only 15 percent of the licensed drivers in the state, they are involved in 29 percent of all fatal alcohol-related crashes.
- According to the National Highway Traffic Safety Administration, motor vehicle crashes are the number one cause of death among youth ages fifteen to twenty.
- According to the Core Institute at Southern Illinois University, 27 percent of college students drive under the influence of alcohol—this is about 2 million college students.
- An estimated 110,000 students between the ages of eighteen and twenty-four are arrested each year for an alcohol-related violation such as public drunkenness or driving under the influence.

According to the Insurance Institute on Highway Safety:

- In 2004, 26 percent of sixteen- to twenty-year-old passenger vehicle drivers fatally injured in crashes had high BACs (0.08 percent or higher).
- The percentage of fatally injured drivers with high BACs was lower among female teenagers (14 percent) than among male teenagers (31 percent).

BAC Levels

- A person is usually "tipsy" or "buzzed" when they have a BAC of around 0.02 to 0.03.
- With a BAC of 0.15 to 0.20 a person is noticeably intoxicated and is severely impaired.
- Heavy drinkers tend to lose consciousness at BAC levels between 0.30 and 0.40.
- A BAC of 0.50 usually results in death.

According to the National Highway Traffic Safety Administration:

- During 2004 the most frequently recorded BAC level of drivers involved in fatal crashes was 0.18.

- About half of all drivers arrested and half of those convicted of DUI have BAC levels of 0.15 or above.
- As of January 1, 2006, thirty-one states have enacted high-BAC laws (laws that impose additional penalties for having high BAC levels). The adopted high BAC levels in these states range from 0.15 to 0.20.
- A person with a BAC level of 0.15 or higher is twenty times more likely than a sober driver to be in a fatal car accident.

Open Container Laws

Open container laws prohibit driving with open containers of alcohol in the vehicle.

According to the National Highway Safety and Traffic Administration:
- States without open container laws experience significantly greater proportions of alcohol-involved fatal motor vehicle crashes than states with open container laws.

According to Mothers Against Drunk Driving
- There is a 5.1 percent decrease in fatal crash rates after states pass an open container law.

Repeat Intoxicated Driver Laws

According to the National Highway Safety and Traffic Administration:
- About one-third of all drivers arrested for DUI have a previous DUI conviction.
- Although many repeat intoxicated drivers continue to drive without a license after the license has been revoked, studies have shown that those who drive tend to drive less frequently and more carefully.
- Thirty-two percent of second-time DUI offenders with suspended licenses were cited for traffic violations or received crash citations during the period their license was suspended.
- Sixty-one percent of third-time DUI offenders with suspended licenses were cited for traffic violations or received crash citations during the period their licenses were suspended.

- A study of ignition interlock devices used in Maryland found that participation in an ignition interlock program decreased the risk of repeat DUI by 65 percent.

Sobriety Checkpoints

- As of January 2006, sobriety checkpoints are allowed in thirty-nine states, the District of Columbia, and Puerto Rico.
- Iowa, Idaho, Michigan, Minnesota, Montana, Oregon, Rhode Island, Texas, Washington, Wisconsin, and Wyoming do not allow sobriety checkpoints.

According to Mothers Against Drunk Driving:

- Sobriety checkpoints can reduce alcohol-related crashes and fatalities by 20 percent.
- Seventy to eighty percent of Americans favor sobriety checkpoint use to combat drunk driving.
- Sobriety checkpoints have been successfully run in California and Ohio with only three to four police officers.
- Checkpoints yield more arrests for DWI/DUI per officer duty-hour than normal patrols.
- Well-conducted sobriety checkpoints generally delay drivers for no more than thirty seconds and cause no traffic problems.

Organizations to Contact

Advocates for Highway and Auto Safety
750 First St. NE, Suite 901
Washington, DC 20002
(202) 408-1711
fax: (202) 408-1699
e-mail: advocates@saferoads.org
Web site: www.saferoads.org

This organization is an alliance of consumer, health and safety groups, and insurance companies that encourages adoption of laws, policies, and programs that save lives and reduce injuries. The group's Web site has information and news on a variety of highway safety issues, including drunk driving and teen driving.

The American Beverage Institute (ABI)
1775 Pennsylvania Ave. NW, Suite 1200
Washington, DC 20006
(202) 463-7110
Web site: www.americanbeverageinstitute.com

ABI is a restaurant trade association. It believes 0.08 BAC is too low and that sobriety checkpoints frighten the casual drinker who would like to dine out and have a drink. The statistics and analysis on ABI's Web site challenge the validity or interpretation of information cited by drunk-driving prevention advocates MADD.

Campaign Against Drunk Driving (CADD)
PO Box 62
Brighouse, West Yorkshire HD6 3YY
0845-123-5541
e-mail: cadd@scard.org.uk
Web site: www.cadd.org.uk

CADD is an organization in Great Britain dedicated to providing support to victims of drunk driving and to promoting stronger drunk-driving laws, including a lower BAC level. Web site can provide sources for drunk driving statistics in Great Britain.

The Century Council
1310 G Street NW, Suite 600
Washington, DC 20005
(202) 637-0077
fax: (202) 637-0079
e-mail: moultone@centurycouncil.org
Web site: www.centurycouncil.org

The Century Council is dedicated to fighting drunk driving and underage drinking by developing and implementing innovative programs and public awareness campaigns. The Web site provides excellent information on studies conducted by Century Council as well as by other organizations. The Century Council's National Hardcore Drunk Driver Project provides excellent information on the problem of repeat offenders with high BAC levels.

Insurance Institute for Highway Safety (IIHS)
1005 N. Glebe Rd., Suite 800
Arlington, VA 22201
(703) 247-1500
fax: (703) 247-1588
Web site: www.iihs.org

IIHS is a scientific and educational organization dedicated to reducing the losses—deaths, injuries, and property damage—from crashes on the nation's highways. IIHS's Web site contains research and statistics on drunk driving and information on laws about drunk driving in all fifty states. This also is the Web site for the Highway Loss Data Institute, whose mission is to compute and publish insurance loss results by car make and model. Both organizations are wholly supported by auto insurers.

MADD Canada
2010 Winston Park Dr., Suite 500
Oakville, ON L6H 5R7
(905) 829-8805

(800) 665-6233
fax: (905) 829-8860
e-mail: info@madd.ca
Web site: www.mad.ca

This group is the Canadian national organization for Mothers Against Drunk Driving (MADD) described below. It has the same aims as MADD and has a searchable database of research abstracts that provides a good source of information on drunk driving in Canada.

Mothers Against Drunk Driving (MADD)
511 E. John Carpenter Fwy., Suite 700
Irving, TX 75062
(800) 438-6233
fax: (972) 869-2206/07
Web site: www.madd.org

MADD's mission is to prevent drunk driving, support victims of drunk drivers, and prevent underage drinking. Its Web site has a search engine and a variety of statistics about drunk driving and information useful for advocacy groups seeking stiffer penalties for drunk driving. MADD's press releases, available on the Web site, keep drunk driving in the public eye.

National Commission Against Drunk Driving (NCADD)
8403 Colesville Rd., Suite 370
Silver Spring, MD 20910
(240) 247-6004
fax: (240) 247-7012
e-mail: info@ncadd.com
Web site: www.ncadd.com

NCADD is a coalition of public and private sector organizations and other concerned individuals who are working together to reduce impaired driving and its tragic consequences. The Web site has a searchable database of abstracts of research studies that make an excellent research resource.

National Highway Traffic Safety Administration (NHTSA)
400 Seventh St. SW
Washington, DC 20590
(888) 327-4236
Web site: www.nhtsa.dot.gov

The NHTSA is a government agency that promotes traffic safety and enforces federal laws concerning highways. The Web site has a search engine and a wealth of information on drunk driving issues and resources that can be used on a local level to promote drunk driving prevention.

Responsibility in DUI Laws, Inc. (RIDL)
PO Box 87053
Canton, MI 48188
e-mail: info@ridl.us
Web site: www.ridl.us

RIDL believes the current trend in DUI laws is aimed at criminalizing and punishing responsible drinkers and has little effect toward curbing drunk driving. RIDL's mission is to educate the public and lawmakers about the misdirection of the current laws, take the steps necessary to get the current laws repealed, and provide alternative suggestions for dealing with the problem of drunk driving. Its Web site has analysis of drunk driving information that questions many of the drunk driving statistics and interpretations of statistics cited by groups like MADD.

Students Against Destructive Decisions (SADD)
Marlborough, MA 01752
(877) SADD-INC
fax: (508) 481-5759
e-mail: info@sadd.org
Web site: www.sadd.org

Originally called Students Against Drunk Driving, SADD's mission later expanded to provide students with the best prevention and intervention tools possible to deal with the issues of underage drinking, other drug use, impaired driving, and other destructive decisions. SADD's Web site has some statistics on teens, drunk driving, and alcohol consumption along with information on how to form local SADD chapters.

The University of North Carolina Highway Safety Research Center
CB# 3430
Chapel Hill, NC 27599
(919) 962-2202 (in NC)
(800) 672-4527
fax: (919) 962-8710
Web site: www.hsrc.unc.edu

The University of North Carolina Highway Safety Research Center has conducted interdisciplinary research aimed at reducing deaths, injuries, and related societal costs of roadway crashes. Alcohol impairment and teen driving are among the areas addressed on its Web site.

U.S. Department of Transportation (DOT)
400 7th St. SW
Washington, DC 20590
(202) 366-400
Web site: www.dot.gov

DOT works to promote fast, safe, efficient, convenient, and accessible transportation in the United States. The Federal Highway Administration and the National Highway Traffic Safety Administration both are agencies of DOT. The department's searchable Web site can be used to access articles and reports of the DOT and other government agencies concerning drunk driving.

For Further Reading

Books

Aaseng, Nathan, *Teens and Drunk Driving*. San Diego: Lucent, 2000. Examines teens and drunk driving, discussing how drinking affects driving ability, who drinks and drives and why, the law and drunk driving, and preventing drunk driving tragedies.

Edwards, Griffith, *Alcohol: The World's Favorite Drug*. New York: St. Martin's, 2000. Examines the role of alcohol in history. Includes good information on the temperance movement in the United States.

Kuen, James S., *Reckless Disregard: Corporate Greed, Government Indifference, and the Kentucky School Bus Crash*. New York: Simon & Schuster, 1994. Details a very famous drunk driving case in which twenty-seven died and thirty-four were injured. The case called public attention to the problem of drunk driving.

Roth, Marty, *Drunk the Night Before: An Anatomy of Intoxication*. Minneapolis: University of Minnesota Press, 2005. Cultural history of drinking from ancient times to the twentieth century.

Thorburn, Doug, *Get Out of the Way! How to Identify and Avoid a Driver Under the Influence*. Northridge, CA: Galt, 2002. The book describes on-road behaviors that suggest a high probability of DUI before becoming tragically obvious. The telltale signs are explained clearly and succinctly in a way that will allow any driver to become a "drunk driver detective."

Periodicals

"ABI: MADD's Roadblock Approach Is Misplaced Anti–Drunk Driving Effort," *Drug Detection Report*, August 5, 2004.

Bahrampour, Tara, "Schools Get Graphic on Safety: Wrecked Cars Remind Teens About Perils of Driving Drunk and Recklessly," *Washington Post*, June 23, 2005.

Balko, Radley, "When Drunk Driving Deterrence Becomes Neo-Prohibition," October 9, 2005. www.cato.org.

Berridge, Virginia, "Why Alcohol Is Legal and Other Drugs Are Not: Virginia Berridge Examines the Relevance of Past Experiences to Current Policy-Making," *History Today*, May 1, 2004.

Bloomberg School of Public Health, "Alcohol Drinkers Three Times as Likely to Die from Injury," AScribe Health News Service, February 10, 2005.

"Breathing Problems: Should Teens Be Required to Take Breathalyzer Tests?" *Current Events*, October 7, 2005.

Caetano, R., and C. McGrath, "Driving Under the Influence (DUI) Among US Ethnic Groups," *Accident Analysis and Prevention*, vol. 37, no. 2, 2005.

Carpenter, C., "How Do Zero Tolerance Drunk Driving Laws Work?" *Journal of Health Economics*, vol. 23, no. 1, 2004.

Christie, Michael, "A Seatbelt That Says You're Too Drunk to Drive: Volvo Device Hits Ignition," *Daily Record*, September 7, 2005.

Cichowski, John, "Drinking and Driving: Should Laws Get Tougher?" *Record*, November 23, 2005.

Cucher, Daniel, "A Proposition to Raise Drinking Age to 25," *University Wire*, October 22, 2002.

Dana, Rebecca, "States Implored to Curb Teen Driving; Graduated Licensing, Limits on Passengers Urged by Safety Groups," *Washington Post*, December 17, 2004.

"Drunk Driving Still a Problem for Maine Motorists, Families; Facts and Figures Mean Nothing to Those Who Suffer," *Portland Press Herald*, February 19, 2004.

"Drunk Driving's Toll: Drinking and Driving Is Deadly. It's Time to Crack Down," *Charlotte Observer*, March 15, 2006.

"Extracurricular Breathalyzer a Step Too Far," *Daily Herald*, September 6, 2005.

"Fewer Drunk Driving Deaths," *Drug Detection Report*, September 2, 2004.

Gilden, James, "Alcohol Figures into Some Young Americans' European Plans," *Internet Traveler*, May 15, 2005.

Greenberg, Morral, and A.K. Jain, "How Can Repeat Drunk Drivers Be Influenced to Change? Analysis of the Association Between Drunk

Driving and DUI Recidivists' Attitudes and Beliefs," *Journal of Studies on Alcohol*, vol. 65, no. 4, 2004.

Greene, Jeffrey W., "Battling DUI: A Comparative Analysis of Checkpoints and Saturation Patrols," *FBI Law Enforcement Bulletin*, January 1, 2003.

Hench, David, "Homeward Bound: Kate Bishop, Confined to Her Home for Paralyzing a Man While Driving Drunk, Tries to Educate Others," *Portland Press Herald*, November 1, 2004.

Klopfer, John, "Lower the Drinking Age," *University Wire*, December 6, 2005.

Landis, Bruce, "Bill Would Widen Interlock Use," *Providence Journal*, January 23, 2006.

Majeur, Jeanne, "Still Driving Drunk: Strict Drunk Driving Laws Don't Do Much Good Unless They Are Vigorously Enforced," *State Legislatures*, December 1, 2003.

Maxwell, Anna, "What Works to Reduce Alcohol-Related Harm and Why Aren't the Policies More Popular?" *Social Policy Journal of New Zealand*, July 1, 2005.

McVicar, Nancy, "Calling While Driving as Dangerous as Driving Drunk," *South Florida Sun-Sentinel*, June 29, 2006.

Meredith, Carl G., "DUI Diary of an 'Innocent' Conviction," *Virginian-Pilot*, January 11, 2004.

Pacific Institute for Research and Evaluation, "Lowering the Drinking Age Increases Car Crashes Among Youth, Study Finds: Injuries, Deaths on the Rise After New Zealand Law Change," AScribe Health News Service, November 28, 2005.

Prescott, Katherine P., and Richard Berman, "Q: Should States Lower the Legal Threshold for Drunk Driving?" *Insight on the News*, July 28, 1997.

"Saab Unveils Alcohol Lock-Out Concept," *New Straits Times*, September 11, 2005.

"Seizing Drunks' Cars Is Needed Safety Step," *Santa Fe New Mexican*, May 2, 2006.

Steptoe, A., J. Wardle, N. Bages, J.F. Sallis, P.A. Sanabria-Ferrand, and M. Sanchez, "Drinking and Driving in University Students: An International Study of 23 Countries," *Psychology & Health*, vol. 19, no. 4. 2004.

"We Have to Work Harder to Keep Drunks Off the Road," *Seattle Post-Intelligencer*, July 6, 2006.

Web Sites

Bomis: The Poems Against Drunk Driving Ring (www.bomis.com/rings/poems). The Web site has links to touching poems posted by people on other sites about their own losses that resulted from drunk driving.

Friends Drive Sober (www.friendsdrivesober.org). The Web site contains a lot of statistics with a specific focus on college students. It also provides information on how college students can form a campus task force to prevent impaired driving. The "factoid" feature on the Web site can provide lots of quick and interesting facts about drunk driving.

Megalaw (www.megalaw.com/top/drunkdriving.php). A collection of law-related Web resources on drunk driving.

Index

accident victims, 56–57
Adkins, Jonathan, 87
alcohol
  age 21 purchasing laws for
    are effective, 51–52
    deter drunk driving, 64
    lives saved by, 66
    promote alcohol use, 69–71
  use of, in American history, 9–10
alcoholics, 27
Alcohol Monitoring Systems, Inc., 17
American Medical Association (AMA), 11
Asbridge, Mark, 74

BAC. *See* blood alcohol levels
Balko, Radley, 32
Ball, Lamar, 89
Berning, Amy, 89
binge drinking
  in Europe, 66
  by U.S. college students, 69
Birch, Glynn R., 18–19
blood alcohol levels (BAC), 11–12
  among young drivers, 50
  traffic fatalities related to, 16–17
  impairment and, 77
  legal reduction of
    is unfair to social drinkers, 82–83
    saves lives, 75
    unintended consequences of, 80–82
    for young drivers, 51
  by number of drinks and weight, 12
  penalties should be based on, 84–85
  state laws on, 17
Breathalyzer Law (Canada), 74, 78
  BAC under, 75
  has saved lives, 77–78
Bush, Jeb, 88

Cato Institute, 32
Chicago Tribune (newspaper), 25
Constitution, U.S., 10
  drunk drivers have lost rights under, 34–37
  see also Fourth Amendment; Fifth Amendment; Sixth Amendment

DeYoung, David J., 91
Diana (princess of Wales), 9, 12–13
Doyle, John, 44
drivers licenses
  revoking, 35
    is ineffective, 57–58
    is deterrent, 61
driving under the influence (DUI)
  among youth, 64
  annual deaths/injuries caused by, 56
  convictions for, 36
  first time offenders, 95–96
  ignition interlock devices reduce, 89
  reasons drivers avoid, 57
  recidivists, 95
drunk drivers, 83
  chronic
    characteristics of, 56
    license suspensions do not deter, 57–58
  difficulty in prosecution of, 17–18
  fines do not deter, 29–30
  with high BAC levels
    checkpoints do not target, 46
    fatalities related to, 16–17
drunk driving. *See* driving under the influence
DUI, *See* driving under the influence

electronic home monitoring, 59, 60–61
El Nasser, Haya, 86
Emerich, Keith, 33
Engs, Ruth, 68
Europe
  binge drinking among youth in, 66
  drinking ages in, 72

fatalities. *See* traffic fatalities
Fatality Analysis Reporting System (FARS), 22–23
Ferguson, Susan, 26
Fifth Amendment, 3435
Flam-Zalcmann, Rosely, 74
Flynn, Katie, 16, 18
Fourth Amendment, 23, 33

Generation Y
  drunk driving among, 28–29
  see also youth

Haas, Ed, 20
Hamilton, Wendy, 26, 31, 87
Hanson, David J., 68
Hingson, Ralph, 29

ignition interlock devices, 35, 36
  are deterrent, 59–60
  California law on, 92
  costs of, to offenders, 87
  effectiveness of, 89
    is questionable, 93–95

growing use of, 88–89
Insurance Institute for Highway Safety (IIHS), 17, 26, 49
International Council on Alcohol, Drugs, and Traffic Safety, 89

Journal of Studies on Alcohol, 52
Journal of the American Medical Association, 22

Larson, Pat, 27
Los Angeles Times (newspaper), 33

Mann, Robert E., 74
Mansfield, Kris, 16, 18
Masten, Scott V., 91
Mather, Increase, 9–10
Mejeur, Jeanne, 15
Michael, Jeff, 29
Michigan v. Sitz (1990), 33, 43
Mineta, Norm, 45–46
Mothers Against Drunk Driving (MADD), 9, 22, 57, 87

National Commission Against Drunk Driving (NCADD), 55
National Hardcore Drunk Driver Project, 84

National Highway Traffic Safety Administration (NHTSA), 11, 39
  BAC levels and, 21, 22, 46
  characteristics used by, 23
  on decline in fatalities, 52
  on age 21 purchasing laws, 66
National Motorists Association (NMA), 12, 79
National Safety Council, 11

O'Connor, Rachel, 90
Ortiz, Felix, 88

Polzin, Lauren Zolecki, 27, 28
Popely, Rick, 25
Prescott, Katherine, 9
Prohibition, 10, 69–70

Rehnquist, William, 33

seat belts, 56
Simon, Steve, 12
Sixth Amendment, 34
sobriety checkpoints
  are effective, 26, 40–42
  catch innocent drivers, 46, 48
  erode 4th Amendment protections, 23
  public approval of, 40
  roving patrols and, 46, 80
  states allowing, 42
  states without, 48

speakeasies, 10
Stoduto, Gina, 74
Supreme Court
  on sobriety checkpoints, 33, 43
  on state drunk driving laws, 34–35
surveys
  on drinking among adults, 10
  on sobriety checkpoints, 40
  of youth, 53

Tashima, Helen N., 91
traffic fatalities, 18, 22, 48
  are declining, 21
    con, 26
  are exaggerated, 24
  due to drunk drivers 16–17
  frequency of, 11
  lowered BAC levels reduce, 75–76
  percentage of
    involving repeat offenders, 26
    involving young drivers, 27–28, 50
    by state, 28

U.S. Public Interest Research Group, 11

Vanek, James, 29–30
vehicle immobilization laws, 59
vehicle seizures, 35
Voas, Robert, 63

Youth, 67, 72-73
  alcohol purchasing by, 53
  binge drinking among
    age 21 laws promote, 71
    in Europe, 66
    by U.S. college students, 69
  prevalence of drunk driving among, 52

zero tolerance laws, 51–52

Picture Credits

Cover, © Brand X Pictures/Alamy
© Bill Bachmamn/Alamy, 41
© Brand X Pictures/Alamy, 81
© Andre Jenny/Alamy, 34
© pymca/Alamy, 70
© Stock Connection Distribution/Alamy, 51
© Transtock, Inc./Alamy, 82
Associated Press, AP, 10(upper), 16, 27, 47, 53, 58, 65, 93
© Jonathan Blair/CORBIS, 94
© Tim Graham/CORBIS, 10(lower)
© Hutchings Stock Photography/CORBIS, 30
© Wally McNamee/CORBIS, 63
© Royalty Free/CORBIS, 14
© George Steinmetz/CORBIS, 23
© Shepard Sharbell/CORBIS SABA, 18
Getty Images, 38
Dom. Poieier/MAXPPP/Landov, 60
Steve Zmina, 21, 36, 57, 66, 72, 77

About the Editor

Mike Wilson is an attorney living in Lexington, Kentucky, author of three children's history books, and edited World Religion and Democracy, two books in the Greenhaven Press series Opposing Viewpoints.

JUV 363.12 D78
Drunk driving

DEC 1 2 2007